VOYEUR VOLUME 2

AN EROTIC ADVENTURE

EROTICA THEMED BUNDLES
BOOK 19

VICTORIA RUSH

VOLUME 19

EROTICA THEMED BUNDLES - BOOK 19

COPYRIGHT

Voyeur Volume 2 © 2024 Victoria Rush

Cover Design © 2023 PhotoMaras

ALSO BY VICTORIA RUSH

Adult Fairytales:

The Enchanted Forest: An Erotic Fairytale

The Land of Giants: An Erotic Fairytale

The Dragon's Lair: An Erotic Fairytale

Witch's Brew: An Erotic Fairytale

The Mage's Spell: An Erotic Fairytale

The Mermaid Lagoon: An Erotic Fairytale

The Coven: An Erotic Fairytale

Rapunzel: An Erotic Fairytale

The Seven Dwarfs: An Erotic Fairytale

The Land of Mutants: An Erotic Fairytale

The Erotic Temple: A Sexy Fairytale (Coming Soon)

Erotica Themed Bundles:

Voyeur: Lesbian Erotica Bundle

Public Affairs: A Lesbian Anthology

Futa Fantasies: The Ladyboy Collection

Threesomes: The Lesbian Collection

Threesomes - Volume 2: The Lesbian Collection

First Time: A Lesbian Anthology

Hedonism: An Erotic Anthology

Switch Hitters: Bisexual Erotica

Taboo Erotica: The Lesbian Series

BDSM: The Lesbian Collection

Party Games: The Erotic Collection

Party Games 2: The Erotic Collection

All Girl 1: Lesbian Erotica Bundle

All Girl 2: Lesbian Erotica Bundle

All Girl 3: Lesbian Erotica Bundle

All Girl 4: Lesbian Erotica Bundle

Erotic Fairytale Bundles:

Clover's Fantasy Adventures: Books 1 - 5

Clover's Fantasy Adventures: Books 6 - 10

Erotic Fantasy:

Pirate's Bounty: A Time Travel Adventure

Wild West: A Time Travel Adventure

Private Riley: A Time Travel Adventure

Cleopatra's Secret: A Time Travel Adventure

Bounty Hunter 2125: A Time Travel Adventure

Ninja Assassin: A Time Travel Adventure

The 300: A Time Travel Adventure

Arabian Nights: An Erotic Fairytale (coming soon...)

Steamy Time Travel Bundles:

Riley's Time Travel Adventures: Books 1 - 5

Lesbian Erotica:

The Dinner Party: Lesbian Voyeur Erotica

The Darkroom: Bisexual Voyeur Erotica

Naked Yoga: Lesbian Transgender Erotica

Nude Cruise: Bisexual Voyeur Erotica

Rush Hour: Taboo Public Sex

The Girl Next Door: First Time Lesbian Erotic Romance

Girls' Camp: Lesbian Group Sex

Wet Dream: Ladyboy Fantasy Erotica

The Convent: Taboo Sex with a Nun

Sex Robot: A Dream Sex Machine

The Personal Trainer: Getting Pumped at the Gym

The Dominatrix: BDSM Lesbian Domination

Webcam Chat: Lesbian Online Sex

Paint Me: A Kinky Bodypainting Workshop

The Toy Party: Girls Sharing Sex Toys

The Costume Party: Strapping One On

Swedish Sauna: Lesbian Group Sex

The Therapist: Taboo Lesbian Erotica

Elevator Shaft: Bisexual Threesomes Erotica

Ladyboy: Lesbian Transgender Erotica

Peep Show: Lesbian Voyeur Erotica

The Dare: Public Sex Erotica

Maid Service: Lesbian Threesomes Erotica

The Hitchhiker: First Time Lesbian Erotica

The Housesitter: Spycam Lesbian Erotica

The Spa: Lesbian Group Orgy

Parlor Games: Blindfold Sex Party

The Exchange Student: First Time Lesbian Erotica

The Hostel: Bisexual Group Erotica

The Harem: Lesbian Erotic Romance

The Orient Express: Lesbian Voyeur Erotica

The First Lady: A Forbidden Lesbian Erotic Romance

The Slave: Lesbian BDSM Erotica

The Masseuse: Lesbian Sensuous Erotica

Too Close for Comfort: Lesbian Forbidden Erotica

Naked Twister: A Wild Party Game

Lexi: The Sex App (Lesbian Fantasy Erotica)

Call Girl: Lesbian Bisexual Threesomes Erotica

Circle Jill: Lesbian Masturbation Workshop

The Viewing Room: Masturbation Voyeur Erotica

Spin the Bottle: A Kinky Party Game

The Hair Salon: Lesbian Voyeur Erotica

Tribadism 1: Girls Only Sex Workshop

Tribadism 2: The Art of Scissoring

Tribadism 3: Threeway Hookups

The Kiss: A Game of Oral Sex

Pledge Week: Sorority Sisters

Carny Games 1: A Wild Sex Party

Carny Games 2: A Kinky Sex Party

Carny Games 3: An Erotic Sex Party

Dreamscape: An Artificial Reality Game

Glory Hole: Guess Who's On the Other Side

Joy Ride: A Late Night Erotic Bus Trip

The Blind Girl: An Erotic Romance(Coming Soon)

Lesbian Erotica Bundles:

Jade's Erotic Adventures: Books 1 - 5

Jade's Erotic Adventures: Books 6 - 10

Jade's Erotic Adventures: Books 11 - 15

Jade's Erotic Adventures: Books 16 - 20

Jade's Erotic Adventures: Books 21 - 25

Jade's Erotic Adventures: Books 26 - 30

Jade's Erotic Adventures: Books 31 - 35

Jade's Erotic Adventures: Books 36 - 40

Jade's Erotic Adventures: Books 41 - 45

Jade's Erotic Adventures: Books 46 - 50

Fifty Shades of Jade: Superbundle

Standalone Stories:

The Polynesian Girl: A Lesbian EroticRomance

For the uninhibited...

WANT TO AMP UP YOUR SEX LIFE?

Sign up for my newsletter to receive more free books and other steamy stuff. Discover a hundred different ways to wet your whistle!

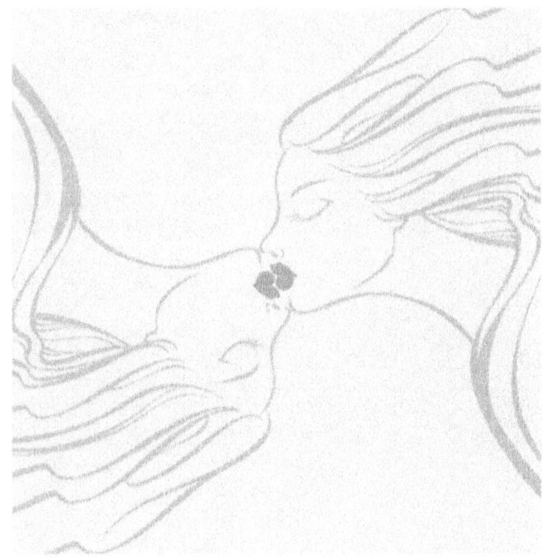

Victoria Rush Erotica

THE HOUSE SITTER

VICTORIA RUSH

1

As I finished packing my bags for my two-week vacation to Bora Bora, my heart pounded with excitement. I hadn't been away from home for this long in years, and I could already feel the warm sea breeze on my face. Even though it was early March in Chicago, I'd chosen to wear light Bermuda shorts and open sandals so I could enjoy the tropical lifestyle the moment I stepped off the plane. I was ready to leave the melting snow and biting wind-chill of the midwestern winter far behind.

But I was anxious for another reason. I was about to leave the security of my valuable home and the care of my beloved tabby cat in the hands of a teenager I barely knew. I'd seen her grow up over the years as the daughter of my best friend, but this was the first time she'd be responsible for managing an entire household on her own. Granted, her mother lived only a half-hour away, but there was still a lot of mischief a high school senior could get into left to her own devices for so long. I had visions of her holding wild house parties and her friends trashing the place while the neighbors looked on disapprovingly as the cops raided the place.

The only comfort I had was knowing I'd be able to monitor the property 24/7 using my recently installed security system. With five

Wi-Fi-enabled cameras installed at key locations in and around the house, I'd be able to watch and listen for any unusual activity directly from my iPhone. I was a bit concerned about invading my housesitter's privacy, but I'd already informed her of the setup and both she and her mother seemed okay with the arrangement.

Besides, it wasn't as if I'd be spying on her in private areas like the bathroom and bedroom. I just wanted to make sure that the main points of ingress and egress were protected and that high-value areas of my house could be watched. I'd had the system installed for *her* safety as much as my own.

Or so I'd convinced myself.

As I carried my suitcases downstairs, I heard the soft chime of the doorbell. I looked at my watch and saw that I had four hours before my flight departure.

Good girl, I thought. She's already demonstrating responsibility by arriving on time for our scheduled briefing. Even though I'd emailed her intricate instructions, there were still a few important details I wanted to go over.

But when I opened the door, I wasn't quite ready for what I saw. The cute freckle-faced teenager I'd known in her youth had blossomed into a beautiful, curvy, full-figured woman. Wearing tight stretch jeans and a form-fitting sweater, she reminded me of the statuesque actress Christina Hendricks from the TV series Mad Men. I hadn't seen her for quite a few months, and she seemed to have a whole new confidence about her.

"Hi Jenny," I stammered, catching my breath. "Please, come in. Do you need some help with your bags?"

"No thanks, Mrs. Jackson," she smiled, lifting her small suitcase, stepping into my vestibule. She had flushed cheeks from the cold weather outside and she rubbed her hands together to warm them up as I closed the door.

"You must be freezing in those light clothes," I said. "Didn't you bring a jacket?"

"I wasn't planning on leaving the house very much," she said. "I've got lots of homework to keep me busy during the school break."

I nodded my head, knowing she was gearing up for college in the fall.

"Yes, I suppose so," I said. "But at least the garage is heated, and you'll have the full use of my car while I'm away if you need anything. So hopefully you'll have minimal exposure to the elements."

"Thanks," Jenny said. "I'll take good care of your property, I promise."

"It'll be good training for college," I smiled. "Is this the first time you've been on your own for this long?"

"Other than the occasional babysitting gig, yes."

"I've stocked up the fridge and left instructions for everything in the kitchen, so hopefully it won't be too much trouble. Why don't you bring your bags and leave them at the bottom of the stairs while I get you up to speed?"

Jenny followed me down the hall and dropped her bags at the landing to my stairs, then I led her into the kitchen and swung open the pantry door.

"The most important thing is making sure Oscar is properly fed and keeping his litter box clean. I've pulled out two cans of cat food and a bag of kibble and placed them on the kitchen island. All the other instructions are on the fridge door."

Oscar jumped up on top of the island when he heard the familiar rustling of his kibble bag, and Jenny rubbed his shoulders while I continued the briefing.

"I give him two scoops of kibble in his dish by the door in the morning and try to keep his water dish at least half-filled with fresh water at all times. Then another half-can of wet food around six p.m. and a few mouthfuls of kibble whenever he seems needy."

"He seems pretty amenable," Jenny said, listening to him purr as she gently stroked his back.

"He's pretty low maintenance," I nodded, happy to see Oscar warming up to her so fast. "Give him a little bit of cuddling a few times a day and he's pretty happy. Let me show you where I keep his litter box."

I led Jenny to my main-floor laundry room and opened a closet door revealing a large bag of cat litter.

"His litter box is under the laundry sink. If you clean it once every couple of days, it will keep the smell under control. Just scoop up any clumps you see with the little ladle and place it in this covered waste can. If it gets full, the trash collection comes every Tuesday and Friday, but honestly it should be fine for the two weeks you're here. If the litter gets low, refill as necessary using this bag."

I pointed to a cat toy resting atop one of the shelves.

"If you feel like playing with him every now and then to keep him from getting bored, he loves playing this little cat-and-mouse game."

I picked up the toy fishing rod and dangled a stuffed mouse above his head while he playfully batted at it. After I placed the device on the dryer, Jenny picked it up and pulled the mouse along the floor in front of Oscar's face as he chased after it. I couldn't help noticing her round ass in her tight jeans as she wiggled her hips to simulate the mouse scurrying along the floor.

"Perfect," I smiled with a slight flush in my face. "You two will be best friends in no time. Of course, you're welcome to use the washer and dryer at your leisure. The controls are pretty self-explanatory."

"I'm used to doing my own laundry, so no problem," Jenny nodded.

I led her back to the kitchen and placed my keys on the island countertop.

"These are the keys to the house and the car. Instructions for the TV remote are on the table beside my sofa. You're also welcome to use my computer in the office if you need to print anything or do some extra homework. The login password is Oscar123."

I glanced into my backyard and motioned to the pool.

"One other thing. I've uncovered the pool a bit early and turned on the water heater, so if you feel like a refreshing swim or want to use the hot tub, feel free any time."

Jenny looked outside and widened her eyes looking at the rippling turquoise water.

"Wow," she said. "I wasn't expecting that. I'm afraid I didn't bring any swim clothes..."

"I've got some swimsuits in my bedroom dresser upstairs. You're welcome to use those." I glanced at Jenny's large breasts and chuckled. "Though I'm not sure you'll fit into them very comfortably."

"I'll find a way to make do," she smiled.

"Okay then," I said, suddenly aware of the twitch in my pussy. "Everything else is pretty self-explanatory, but if you have any questions or run into any trouble you can text me on my phone. I should have it with me most of the time, but if there's an emergency you can also call my neighbor Betty, whose number is on the fridge."

"I hope you won't be looking at your phone *too* much while you're on vacation," Jenny smiled. "Isn't that the whole point of going on vacation? To get away from all those everyday troubles?"

"Of course," I said, pulling my cell phone out of my purse. "I don't intend to, but I wanted to remind you that I've got cameras set up in various places throughout the house to keep an eye on things. I'll be checking in periodically to make sure you're not having any wild parties or burning the place down."

"Not to worry, Mrs. Jackson," Jenny chuckled. "Between the pool, the TV, and the computer, I've got plenty of other things to keep me amused."

I smiled at her, admiring her voluptuous figure.

"There are no cameras in the private areas like as the bedroom and washrooms, so you don't have to worry about your personal privacy." I pointed outside the kitchen door, where a small wireless camera hung from the eavestrough. "But just so you know, one camera keeps an eye on the backyard, and there's also one at each of the exit doors, and one at the top and bottom of the central stairway, all of which can pan and tilt to provide wide coverage of each area. So you might want to keep your clothes on while you're scampering around the house."

"No problem with the cameras," Jenny smiled. "I'm used to having my parents keeping close tabs on me already."

"I'll bet," I said, trying not to undress her with my eyes. "You must be dying to head off to college in a few months. All those cute boys and toga parties–you'll think you'd died and gone to heaven."

"I'm not really into all that..." Jenny said, shrugging her shoulders.

"Not even *boys*? There'll be a whole new set of rules once you get onto campus."

"We'll see," Jenny said, glancing at my cleavage in my tight cotton blouse. "I'm sure there'll be plenty of other distractions when I get there."

"Um, yes," I said, momentarily taken aback by her sudden change in demeanor. I heard a honk from the driveway and glanced at my watch. "That must be my taxi. Did you have any more questions before I head off for the airport?"

"I think I'm good to go," Jenny said. "Enjoy your trip and don't worry about Oscar or your house. Everything will be just like you left it when you come back."

"Thanks, Jenny," I said, leaning in to give her a peck on the cheek. "Thanks again for looking after things while I'm away. I've transferred four hundred dollars to your account for the initial deposit. I'll pay the second installment when I return."

"Sounds great," Jenny said, cradling a purring Oscar in her arms. "But if everything turns out to be *this* easy, I might have to issue a refund."

"You're going to need every penny you can earn for college," I said. "It's the least I can do."

I carried my bags out to the driveway and the taxi driver placed them in the trunk, then I nestled into the back seat. It wasn't until I sat down that I realized how wet my panties had become. I wasn't sure if it was the feel of Jenny's skin on my lips that had gotten my juices flowing, or her comment about having other distractions at college. Had her glance at my cleavage projected an interest in something other than *boys*?

Either way, something told me that I'd be checking my phone more often than either of us expected while I was on my little South Pacific excursion.

2

———

By the time I checked in for my flight and cleared through security at the airport, it was already starting to get dark. When I got to the waiting area at my departure gate, I picked up a magazine and tried to distract myself while waiting for the flight to board. But I couldn't stop thinking about Jenny. I was absolutely floored by her transformation from a skinny freckle-faced freshman to a stunning, statuesque high school senior. Not only did she have a figure that made my mouth water, but some of her reactions suggested she was just as interested in me as I was with her.

Did her comment about not being into boys and her frequent glances at my cleavage signal she was attracted to women, like me? And when I mentioned that she might not fit into my bathing suit and she responded by saying that she'd find a way to 'make do', did that mean she was intending to swim in her underwear or–God forbid–in the *buff*?

The more I thought about it, the wetter my panties became as I squirmed uncomfortably in my chair. I glanced up at the display board behind the gate agent's desk and saw that I still had fifteen minutes before the plane began boarding.

What the fuck, I murmured, pulling my phone out of my purse, tapping on the home security app. It won't hurt to check up on her before I depart for the first leg of my flight to Hawaii. If only to make sure Oscar's water bowl is filled.

Yeah, *right*, I smiled, knowing full well that I just wanted to catch another glimpse of her sexy body.

When the app opened, it showed two side-by-side panes displaying the camera locations inside the house. Seeing no sign of Jenny in either picture, I tapped on each one and toggled my finger across the screen to angle the camera to pan the upstairs and down-stairs living areas.

Okay, I said, tilting my head. *Maybe she's in the bedroom or the bath-room getting ready to turn in.*

I waited a few minutes, but still seeing no sign of activity, I swiped my thumb to the left to view the two cameras covering the outside doors. She wouldn't have any reason to be outside in the cold weather, unless she'd stepped outside to have a smoke. But she didn't strike me as the type. Shaking my head in dismay, I swiped to the last two images displaying views of the backyard and the garage.

Still no sign of Jenny.

What the hell, I cursed. Where is she hiding? She couldn't have taken off so soon after I'd left. The car was still parked in the garage, so I knew she hadn't gone out for more provisions.

I was just about to tap the playback feature on the inside cameras to track her previous movement when I noticed a shadowy figure moving around the pool image. A curvy girl wearing a terry-cloth robe walked toward the shallow end of the basin, then dropped her robe on the patio and stepped into the steaming water.

"*Holy shit!*" I exclaimed, recognizing her hourglass figure and her long, corkscrew hair. *She's naked! And she's going to skinny dip in my pool!*

The outdoor security camera had detected her movement and turned on the security lamp, illuminating her body like a pale appari-tion against the reflecting surface of the pool. Covering her breasts with crossed arms over her chest, she slowly lowered herself into the water then began doing gentle breast strokes across the thirty-foot-long pit.

As I watched her silvery body gliding through the water like a translucent nymph, I suddenly became aware of the moisture building up between my legs. Even though I could only see the back of her body partially obscured by the swirling water, I could clearly make out the cleft in her ass and the exquisite curvature of her hips as she flapped her legs in and out in a gentle whipping motion.

Jesus Christ, I panted, imagining she was scissoring her legs against something *else* right now.

When she reached the end of the pool and turned around to swim the opposite length, I could see her pretty face illuminated by the bright spotlight as her head bobbed up and down in the shimmering water.

Oh my God, I muttered under my breath, scarcely believing what I was seeing.

I began to spread my legs unconsciously, imagining her burying her face in my pussy as I watched her beautiful ass rising and falling in the tumbling surf. I placed two fingers on the screen and pinched them together, zooming in on her figure slicing through the water. As she swam back and forth across the pool, I traced her motion by drawing my finger slowly across the screen to turn the camera in lock-step with her movement.

I was so mesmerized by the intoxicating scene on my phone, I barely heard the announcement over the public address system for the last call to board my plane. I looked up, and noticing the diminishing line of passengers streaming onto the jet bridge, I picked up my bags and scurried to the end of the queue.

Fuck! I cursed under my breath, trying to balance my iPhone in my hand while I fumbled with my boarding pass.

I just prayed that I'd be able to access the airport's Wi-Fi signal from inside the plane so I wouldn't have to miss another second of watching her sexy figure.

When I nestled into my seat by the window, I turned my body away from my seatmates and pulled my phone close to my breast so I could watch her without any further interruption. The last thing I needed was for someone to catch me leering at her like I was watching some kind of porn video. But just as Jenny paused by the pool-side ladder preparing to lift herself out of the water, the flight attendant announced over the p.a. system that we had to turn off our electronic devices in preparation for take-off.

You've got to be kidding me, I cursed as I watched Jenny reach up onto the handles.

"Madam?" a flight attendant said, leaning over the aisle. "Please turn off your phone and connect your seat belt. We're about to take off."

I peered up at her with my mouth agape, as if supplicating divine intervention. The timing couldn't have been worse. Just as I tapped the power button on the side of my phone, I saw the top of Jenny's dripping breasts rise out of the pool before the screen faded to black. Gritting my teeth in frustration, I checked the information folder in the back pocket of the seat in front of me to learn how to connect to the airplane's inflight Wi-Fi network. I didn't want to miss one more unnecessary second of spying on this sexy vixen if I could avoid it. Even if she'd gotten dressed by the time I got back online, I could still use the replay button to watch the entire scene from start to finish over and over.

Thank God for modern technology, I said to myself, noticing a large wet spot had formed in the front of my shorts.

Forty-five agonizing minutes later, after the plane had reached cruising altitude, I heard a chime and looked up to see that the seat belt sign had been turned off. It was now okay to power back up my electronic devices. I pressed the power button on my phone, tapping my foot impatiently while I waited for the home screen to light up.

When I saw the familiar apps appear on the screen, I tapped the settings icon then clicked the Wi-Fi function to join the air carrier's proprietary inflight service. They were charging an outrageous $24.99 for a full-flight pass, but at this point I would have paid ten times that amount to get back online. After entering my credit card information and agreeing to the terms, I saw the three delta-shaped bars alight on the top left-hand side of my phone screen.

Okay, we're back in business, I huffed, clicking the home security app until it opened up to the pool-cam view. But when the image appeared, there was no longer any sign of Jenny anywhere in the backyard.

Of course she would have gone back indoors after coming out of the pool, I said to myself. *It's freezing cold at this time of the day in Chicago!*

I was about to tap the replay button so I could watch her naked body slicing through the water again when my finger paused over the glass.

Unless...

Could she have jumped in the hot tub to relax and stay warm after her late evening swim? Could I be that lucky?

I swiped my thumb down to tilt the camera closer to the front of the house, and my heart skipped a beat when I saw Jenny submerged in the churning water with her arms outstretched over the rim. Her body was turned away from the neighbors' yards, directly facing the camera. The top of her tits poked out of the swirling water like two pink balloons, dancing atop the churning eddy.

She had a quiet, blissful look on her face, but I could see her body shifting under the opaque surface of the water. For a moment, I thought it was just the action of the powerful jets pushing against her body from all directions. But there was something about the way she was moving her shoulders and adjusting her position on the seat that led me to believe there was something more going on.

Could she possibly be...?

I knew from plenty of personal experience just how pleasurable it was to position the jets directly in front of my pussy. With the powerful rush of water flowing over my clit, there was nothing quite so heavenly as the feel of the warm water caressing my most sensitive part. When Jenny lowered her hands under the water and angled her arms toward her crotch, there was no longer any doubt.

She was playing with herself under the water!

As I watched her lean her head back against the top of the hot tub and her mouth begin to part open, I suddenly felt a rush of heat and wetness to my own aching pussy.

She certainly didn't waste any time making herself comfortable in my house, I smiled.

But I could tell from her position in the tub that she was missing the ideal placement to receive the most direct stimulation.

Move two feet to your left! I wanted to shout at her while I stared at my phone screen. *There's a jet perfectly positioned to stimulate your clit! You haven't lived until you've come from one of those things!*

I remembered that I'd added a two-way audio feature to each of the cams so I could send a warning message to any potential burglars caught by my motion sensors. For a brief moment, I considered turning it on to encourage her to take full advantage of the hot tub's special features. But this was no *burglar*–this was my young housesitter who must have thought I was far out of earshot by now flying over the Pacific Ocean.

Besides, even if I could reach out to her this way, how could I possibly hope to carry on such an intimate conversation without attracting the suspicion of my fellow passengers sitting only inches away?

But it didn't take long for Jenny to figure it out. Her arms stretched out to her sides as she searching for the precise location of each of the water nozzles. When she leaned forward a few inches and felt the jet shooting up from the edge of the bench a few seats over, she froze for a moment as her eyes widened in excitement. It only took a few seconds for her to move directly over the pulsating stream as she slumped her body lower into the water.

Suddenly, her mouth gaped open as she felt the powerful jet pulsing against her sensitive nub. I knew immediately what she was feeling, and I ached to be lying next to her, feeling her body shaking as she reveled in the rising pleasure administered by the powerful spray. She tilted her head further back against the rim, then her elbows flared out from her sides as she squeezed her tits under the swirling water.

Fuck me, I cursed, wishing it were *my* hands caressing her gorgeous melons instead of her own. I dreamed how I'd ravage her in the sensuous whirlpool while hidden from the prying eyes of my neighbors under the cloak of the swirling water.

I sat captivated as Jenny's mouth gaped progressively wider from the intense pleasure building inside her. When her climax finally washed over her, her head began jerking back and forth while her face scrunched up into the most exquisite form of ecstasy. I almost came along with her, squeezing my thighs tightly together trying to keep my body from writhing in sympathy with her next to my oblivious seat mates.

After she stopped trembling in the swirling water, Jenny lay back against the seat of the hot tub and slumped her shoulders in delirious exhaustion. She had the cutest flush on her face, and for a brief moment, I thought she glanced up at the security camera perched only a few feet away from the tub.

Had she suspected that I was watching her the whole time? Did she notice the movement of the camera as I traced her movement in the pool and the hot tub? Or heard the soft whirring of the camera as I zoomed in on her face when she came?

If so, what was already the most stimulating thing I'd witnessed in a long time, suddenly became even more arousing. I needed to release my pent-up sexual tension, and fast. I peered over at the lavatory sign nearest me and noticed that it was vacant. I waited a few minutes until Jenny stepped out of the hot tub, revealing her glorious glistening body, before I asked to be excused.

The moment I locked the lavatory door behind me, I tore off my clothes and thrust three fingers deep inside my sopping pussy, fucking myself furiously. It must have taken less than ten seconds for me to pop off with the most powerful orgasm I'd had in months. As I stood quivering over the sink with my hand embedded in my snatch, I looked up at the mirror and smiled.

I suddenly knew that I wouldn't be so alone on this trip after all.

3

When I returned to my seat, I switched over to the indoor cams and noticed that Jenny had gone upstairs, flitting back and forth between the master bedroom and bath. She'd changed into flannel pajamas with a Little Mermaid pattern, and I smiled at the contrast of the girly cartoon images with her sexy, curvy figure. The upstairs camera was installed at the top of the stairs, but she'd left the bedroom door ajar just enough for me to angle the camera to see the edge of the bed.

When she emerged from the bathroom, she picked up a book from the nightstand and propped up the pillows to provide a comfortable reading position. Then she sat down on the bed and began reading with her legs crossed over one another. As she wiggled her bare toes while she read, I zoomed in the camera to examine her face more closely.

Her auburn hair fell softly against her pale cheeks in gentle ringlets, highlighting her speckled cheekbones. She had large eyes with brilliant green irises, framed by dark eyebrows arching seductively over long lashes. And her slender nose had a slight upturn at the end, accentuating her puffy rosebud lips and cleft chin. Wearing virtually no makeup, she looked like a fashion doll from a Bergdorf Goodman department store.

The perfect model of young, sensual beauty, I thought.

While she read her book, her gaze stayed focused just below the line of sight of the camera down the hall. As much as I wanted to zoom out to take in more of her breathtaking body, I was afraid the noise might attract her attention and she'd catch me spying on her again. But after a while, she placed the book beside her on the bed and peered around my bedroom, looking for another distraction.

Much to my horror, she leaned over and pulled open the drawer to my bedside night stand. The noise of the drawer gave me an opportunity to zoom back out, and I saw her eyes widen as she peered inside at the contents. I'd thought about hiding my sex toys in another location, but I hadn't imagined she'd be bold enough to go fishing around in my personal effects.

Cheeky girl, I smiled, noticing my breathing rate becoming more raspy.

I kept a whole treasure trove of toys next to the bed, and it must have looked like a veritable candy store to a young teenager just turning the corner into adulthood. She pulled out each device one at a time, examining it closely before placing it on the side of the bed beside her.

The first one was the long and sturdy Magic Wand, my trusty industrial-strength vibrator that delivered a powerful and sustained jolt directly to the clitoris. She held the handle vertically in her left hand and gripped the flexible ball at the top, bending it forward and back with her other hand. Then she pulled out my tiny Pocket Rocket and twisted the end, feeling the nubby head beginning to buzz softly in her hand. When she reached in and removed the salami-sized, two-sided silicone dildo that I used whenever I had a special friend over, I grimaced in embarrassment. She grasped the double-headed penis at each end and bent it forward and back into a U-shape, pinching her eyebrows and shaking her head in dismay.

It must have been a shock to her young sensibilities to discover all the naughty ways a woman could stimulate herself with the wide assortment of sex aids on the market. Or maybe she was just trying to fathom how the demure Mrs. Jackson, who she'd known since child-hood, had become such a perverted sex addict.

Not so demure now, am I little girl? I smiled, feeling my juices begin-ning to flow again in my tight Bermuda shorts.

She reached back into the drawer and pulled out a strange-looking device that looked like a balled fist with two fingers pointing up in a V-shape. Jenny held up my familiar JimmyJane vibrator and inserted her finger between the two appendages. Then she tapped the button on the base and smiled as the little digits fluttered against her hand.

Mmm, yes, I nodded toward the screen. *It feels even better when you place your clit between the vibrating fingers.*

I was getting increasingly worked up watching my young hous-esitter play with each of the devices, wondering when she was going to try them in the manner they were intended.

She placed the JimmyJane vibrator down on the mattress, then removed a U-shaped object from the drawer and looked at it with a wrinkled brow. She grasped the two ends of the We-Vibe toy and gently flexed it open a few inches. Then she began tapping the buttons on the outside of the device to feel the different vibration settings on each side.

Did she even know which end to put inside? I wondered. She didn't look like she'd had much experience using vibrators. For all I knew, she'd only seen those hard plastic phallic-shaped dildos still prominently displayed in most sex shop windows.

At least she's got a full two weeks to experiment with them, I smiled.

Knowing the best was yet to come, I saw her lean over and extract one of my favorite sex toys, the Rabbit. Shaped like an oversize erect penis, it had a transparent shaft with circulating beads and a protruding thumb-shaped arm with two soft silicone rabbit ears that fluttered against the clitoris. Jenny picked it up and tapped each of the control buttons on the base, watching with amazement as the head of the dildo wobbled like a spinning top while the chrome beads rotated in the middle of the shaft and the rabbit ears fluttered softly against her palm.

Yeah, girl, I smiled. *That one will put you over the top in no time.*

I was intrigued why Jenny hadn't started to experiment with any of the toys by removing her clothes, but I was thrilled that she was showing so much interest in my special collection.

She turned her head toward the open drawer and pinched her eyebrows, peering at the last item in the drawer. When she pulled it out, I smiled, recognizing the distinctive shape of the Ose vibrator. Shaped like a giant flexed finger with a flat base harboring a mysterious hole, she must have wondered how in God's name it worked. But as she began tapping the buttons on the base of the unit, her eyes widened as she watched the long finger begin to flex in a come-hither motion.

But it wasn't until she pressed the button controlling the *lower* part that her eyes really opened in shock and amazement. As it began to pulse in her hand, she drew it closer and squinted at the little hole, watching it pucker in and out like some kind of animatronic mouth. Which is exactly what it was designed to simulate. This was one of my favorite vibrators for exactly that reason, and for a moment I was disappointed that I hadn't packed it for my trip.

But when I saw Jenny pull down her pajama bottoms and spread her knees apart, I quickly forgot about my own needs as I zoomed in to inspect her sex. I gasped when I saw that she'd shaved herself entirely bare, and my pussy spasmed when I saw her glistening pink folds framing her pretty flower.

When she picked up the Ose vibrator and pointed the finger toward her hole, I shifted uncomfortably in my narrow airplane seat, dying to rip off my clothes and spread my legs far apart while I fucked myself watching her. When she inserted the wand into her slit, I groaned audibly, and the woman sitting next to me turned her head, momentarily distracted from the book she was reading.

But when Jenny thrust the device deep into her pussy and tapped the buttons to activate the two human-like functions, I sat up and cleared my throat, trying to keep myself composed. But the rivers of lubrication running down the inside of my thighs made it clear I was anything but composed. I pulled a magazine out of the seat flap in front of me and placed it on my lap to conceal the rapidly darkening wet spot in the crotch of my shorts, turning the phone screen even further away from the prying eyes of the passengers around me. Even though I'd be absolutely mortified if anyone caught me watching the video, there was no way in hell I could stop now, even if the air marshal tried to force me to put it away. They'd have to send in a virtual *army* to wrench this live feed out of my hands.

With the Ose vibrator now pulsing at full speed against Jenny's pussy, she pulled her knees up closer toward her chest and spread her legs further apart. The sight of the fluttering object planted between her legs as she threw her head back against the pillows was driving me insane with desire. But when she unbuttoned the top of her pajamas and began twisting the teats on her voluptuous tits, I couldn't take it anymore.

I excused myself once again, saying I had an upset stomach, and headed back to the lavatory with my phone in hand. As I waited impatiently for the occupant to come out, I inserted my earbuds into the port on the bottom of my phone and tapped the screen to engage the audio function. I could hear Jenny moaning into my ear, and I flapped my legs impatiently, desperately wanting to get into the private room where I could relieve myself.

When the passenger finally opened the door and began to step out, I practically ran him over squeezing into the chamber, slamming the door shut. I placed the phone on top of the sink and pulled my shorts down to my ankles and thrust two fingers into my snatch, pulling the base of my hand hard up against my throbbing clit. As I watched Jenny's knees beginning to flutter with increasing urgency and a deep flush begin to spread over the top of her bosom, I couldn't hold it any longer. As my orgasm washed over me like a tidal wave, I gushed all over my hand and fingers, shaking like I was having an epileptic seizure.

Soon after, Jenny's body also began to convulse as she groaned in the throes of her own powerful climax. As I watched her firm melons bouncing on her chest and her face flush a deep shade of crimson, I moaned along with her until we were both completely spent and exhausted. Then I peered down at my dripping thighs and drenched shorts lying on the floor, wondering how I'd ever be able to return to my seat in such a messy condition. There was no way I could wear these same shorts drenched in my lubrication and God knows how many other people's dried urine from the lavatory floor. There was only one way out of here.

Opening the door a crack, I waited until a female flight attendant passed by, then I quietly called out to her. She turned toward me with a puzzled look and came closer to my door.

"I'm so sorry to bother you about this," I said. "But I've had a bit of an accident and I'm afraid I won't be able to wear these shorts again for the rest of the flight."

She widened her eyes and nodded knowingly. Apparently, I wasn't the only passenger who'd run into this predicament before.

"Can I ask you a huge favor?" I said. "Could you retrieve my carry-on bag from the overhead storage compartment above seat 15F? It's tan colored and has a name tag for J. Jackson."

"No worries, Mrs. Jackson," she said. "I'll be back with your bag in just a moment."

When she returned with my case, I placed it on top of the small vanity and wiped down my legs with a moist towelette. Then I stepped out of my soiled shorts and threw them in the waste receptacle.

I won't be needing those anymore, I murmured to myself. The hard part would be keeping my dick in my pants for the *rest* of the flight to Hawaii. I knew that I'd have to find another distraction to keep me busy so I didn't soil another pair of shorts.

No more Jenny videos until I get to my own private room, I said.

But my mind was already swimming with all the new entertainment possibilities over the course of the next two weeks.

Who needs tropical beaches and chilled mai tai's when you've got the most beautiful, sexy lingerie model at your beck and call whenever you need her?

4

———

After changing into fresh clothes, I returned to my seat by the window. Even though I was dying to see what Jenny would do next, I dared not reopen the camera app for fear of making another mess. For the rest of the flight to Hawaii, I kept myself distracted watching a movie. A very tame, family-oriented movie. I didn't want to risk viewing another sexy scene that might rekindle my new obsession with my young housesitter.

When we landed in Hawaii, I had to change planes for the next leg of my flight to Bora Bora, so there wasn't any time to check the home security monitors during the brief stopover. By the time I boarded the aircraft, I was so exhausted, I slept the rest of the way to my final destination. When I landed in the archipelago, I took a taxi to my hotel, where a porter escorted me to an overwater bungalow overlooking a turquoise lagoon. I hadn't eaten for eight hours, so I unpacked my bags then headed to the dining room for a sumptuous seafood dinner.

By the time I returned to my room half-intoxicated on margaritas, I was ready to power up my phone and resume watching my new favorite playmate. But with the five-hour time difference between Bora Bora and Chicago, Jenny was already fast asleep, nestled under the warm covers of my bed. It hardly mattered though, since by now I had almost a full day's worth of video to play back any time I wanted.

I tapped the home monitoring app on my phone and toggled back to the upstairs view. I'd left the camera pointed in the direction of the bedroom, so I hoped there'd be plenty more footage of Jenny amusing herself with my toys. But I was disappointed to see that after coming so hard using the Ose vibrator, she'd put the rest of the instruments away before turning in.

I guess after having two powerful back-to-back orgasms, she needed a rest, I smiled. *Or maybe she was just pacing herself, leaving room to enjoy the other devices another day.*

I came three more times replaying the erotic scenes from the hot tub and my bedroom, over and over. When I finally satiated my lust, I took a relaxing dip in my room's private plunge pool, watching the sun set over the quiet lagoon.

I could get used to this, I thought, taking in the blissful scene.

The only thing missing was a partner to enjoy it with. Maybe I'd bring Jenny back with me next time. The only problem was her mother, who just happened to be my best friend. I didn't want to risk damaging our longstanding relationship. Even if Jenny *had* recently turned eighteen and could make her own decisions.

I fell asleep that night feeling the warm ocean breeze wafting through my veranda window, dreaming of Jenny's naked body gliding through the coral waters of my lagoon. When I woke up, it was already past noon Chicago time, and I flipped over my phone to see what she was up to. I found her sitting at the kitchen island with some school books propped open, making notes in her journal.

Good girl. You don't want to waste your entire spring break playing around the house. You'll need good marks to get into your choice of college in the fall. There'll be plenty of other distractions to keep you amused when you get there.

I walked down to the breakfast bar in the hotel and helped myself to a large serving of eggs Benedict with a side of fresh pineapple and lox. I almost felt sorry leaving Jenny with a fridge full of microwave dinners and pre-cooked casseroles. But something told me she'd find *other* ways to keep herself satisfied while I was away.

I needed to find something to keep my mind off what was happening back home, so I signed up for a snorkeling expedition to a nearby reef. When we arrived there, I marveled at the variety of colorful sea creatures, from striped angelfish to iridescent snapper and giant speckled grouper. I loved swimming among the docile nurse sharks and stingrays, even hitching a brief ride on a large sea turtle. After returning to my room and noticing that I was already a bit sunburned, I pulled off my wet bathing suit and propped myself up in my bed.

When I checked in on Jenny, at first I couldn't see any sign of her in the main rooms of the house or in the backyard. It took a few minutes of angling the upstairs and downstairs cams before I saw her seated in my office, quietly tapping on my keyboard. Although the door was slightly ajar, the line of sight from the ceiling-mounted camera to the office only allowed me to see half of her body.

I remembered leaving my login code if she needed to print anything, but the audio feed didn't indicate any sign of activity other than soft tapping on the keyboard. I hesitated for a moment, thinking I'd give her some peace and quiet and check back later in the evening. Maybe I'd catch her using another one of my sex toys when it was closer to bedtime.

But then I remembered I had *another* app on my phone that provided direct access to my home computer. It was useful when I needed to access important files remotely, but I hadn't used it for a long time. I clicked on the app, and it opened showing my live screen with Jenny's cursor hovering near the top of the web browser. She clicked on the bookmarks tab and began scrolling through my list of saved web addresses.

Forgetting that I'd arranged everything into themed folders, I was mortified when she clicked on the folder for my favorite lesbian porn videos. I used these whenever I felt particularly horny and needed a distraction, but I never intended for anyone *else* to find my private stash. She double-clicked on a link labeled *hot tribbing*, and a window opened showing two naked girls scissoring on an oversize bed. Jenny tapped on the speaker icon at the bottom of the screen and slid the volume bar to the right, and I heard soft moaning wafting out into the hall.

Unsure if it was Jenny's voice or the sounds of the girls on the video, I toggled back to the camera monitoring app. Jenny's left leg was spread far apart with her jeans pulled down to her ankles as she rolled her hips sensuously on the chair. Unable to see what she was doing from the rear position of the camera and with her back turned away from me, I cursed at my inability to watch her more closely. Desperately wanting to see what she was doing while she watched the video, I scanned the remote access menu and noticed a camera icon.

When I clicked the button, my iPhone screen divided into a split window with the tribbing video on one side and Jenny's face on the other. I could only see the top half of her body from the fixed position of the webcam atop my laptop, but that was more than enough. Her cheeks were flushed as she squeezed one of her breasts with her right hand and extended her other arm between her legs in a rhythmic motion.

Holy fuck! I groaned. She was playing with herself while watching a lesbian porn video!

There was no longer any doubt in my mind that she was sexually attracted to women. As I watched her face twist into increasing contortions of pleasure, my eyes darted back and forth between the scene playing out on the porn video and the expression on her face. As the girls on the video began rubbing their pussies together more vigorously, I suddenly heard a familiar buzzing sound coming from the background.

Was she fucking herself with one of my vibrators while she watched the video?

I switched back to the security camera view, but all I could see was Jenny's left leg shaking while her free arm pumped something between her legs. Suddenly overcome with desire, I rushed over to my suitcase and pulled out the one vibrator I'd had the foresight to pack for the trip–my trusty Lelo G-spot stimulator. I thrust the gently curved rod into my snatch and turned the vibration setting up high as I flipped back to the screen monitoring app.

I could hear Jenny moaning along with the two girls on the video as her oversize melons began to tremble from the rising pleasure emanating within her. When the girls suddenly locked their hips, pulling each other tightly toward one another screaming in unison, Jenny's mouth gaped apart, and she uttered a deep guttural groan. With her body jerking forward and back in rhythmic contractions, I grabbed my long dildo with two hands and clamped down on it as I came hard along with Jenny.

It must have taken a full minute for both of us to stop spasming and cumming from the erotic scene we'd both witnessed. I smiled at the irony of getting off watching Jenny while she watched the girls on the video. My mind reeled with all the possibilities for engagement between the two of us when I returned home. Suddenly I realized Jenny was no longer just an innocent high school student, but a fully developed woman, ready to experiment with all the different ways of satisfying her sexual curiosity.

Fortunately for me, Jenny was far from finished quenching her desire for the evening. I saw her right hand move back to the cursor, and she tapped on the progress bar to return to the middle of the video. As it began replaying, she slid the slider slowly to the right until it reached the part where the two girls began pulling their bodies together in preparation for their mutual orgasm.

Jenny peered down, and I heard a deeper kind of throbbing sound emanating from between her legs. As the girls in the video began moaning more loudly, she moved both of her hands between her legs, pounding her pussy with hard jerking motions. I couldn't be sure which vibrator she was using, but the sight of her fucking herself while watching the two girls soon had me thrusting my Lelo vibrator back inside my own pussy. As the girls moved closer to their moment of climax, Jenny's face scrunched up into a painful grimace.

She seemed to be waiting for them to cum once again before she opened the taps. When they finally did, her orgasm was even stronger as she wailed in unison with the girls, jerking her arms forcefully against her body and her compressed tits as she quivered in the office chair. I screamed along with her, feeling my juices spraying out the sides of my pulsating pussy all over my wet thighs and ass.

After Jenny recovered from her second powerful orgasm, she closed the porn site and flipped the laptop cover closed. No longer being able to see her directly, I switched over to the hall cam view, watching her pull up her jeans as she raised herself from the chair. Then she turned around and exited the office, walking toward the stairs. In her right hand, I could see the familiar outline of my purple Rabbit vibrator with its distinctive protruding ears.

I smiled as I watched her head back upstairs to return the vibrator to my nightstand.

That's it, baby, I said. *Take your time trying out each of my special toys. Neither of us is going anywhere for the next two weeks.*

5

———————

J enny went to sleep soon after watching the lesbian video, and I decided to go for a relaxing swim in the lagoon to wind down. Between the day's snorkeling activity, a little too much sun, and multiple orgasms watching Jenny on constant replay, I slept like a baby that night. When I woke the following morning, she was back at the kitchen table doing her homework, so I went for another long breakfast at the hotel restaurant.

Since Jenny seemed to be preoccupied with her studies, I decided to make the best use of my time by taking a sailing tour of the island. Wearing a long-sleeved linen shirt, capri pants, and plenty of sunscreen, I wasn't taking any chances at getting more sunburned. With Jenny becoming increasingly bold with her sexual escapades back home, I wanted to make sure I could enjoy watching her without any distractions.

I was surprised how large the island was, taking us more than six hours to circumnavigate the atoll in our sleek, forty-foot catamaran. Formed by an extinct volcano, lush green hillsides rose steeply above the water to over two thousand feet above sea level. I marveled at how clear the water was as I gazed at the endless variety of colorful fish through the sturdy nets joining the two hulls. But by the time we'd finished our mid-day picnic on a secluded beach, I was ready to get out of the sun and back to the relative tranquility of my private cabin.

When the sailboat returned to the hotel, it was already early evening Chicago time, and I was eager to see what mischief Jenny had gotten into while I was away. After I got back to my bungalow, I turned on my phone and saw her taking a swim in the backyard pool wearing a skimpy cream-colored bikini. Looking like a young Ursula Andress from the famous beach scene in the James Bond movie *Dr. No*, she looked even *more* mouth-watering partially covered up.

But this time she wasn't alone. She'd invited a young friend over, and as the two girls splashed each other's faces in the pool, my pussy twitched at the sight of the two scantily clad teens. When they got out of the pool, they moved over to the hot tub, where Jenny encouraged her friend to try out the special seat she'd used the previous day. I could see the look of surprise on her girlfriend's face when she felt the gush of the underwater jet flowing between her legs, but she didn't seem interested in staying there long enough to get properly aroused.

Whether she felt self-conscious stimulating herself in front of her girlfriend or Jenny had warned her that I could be monitoring the property, I wasn't sure. But either way, I enjoyed watching the girls' pretty faces as the swirling water flowed over the tops of their bikini-clad bodies. Just to be safe, I kept the camera zoomed out and the audio turned off for fear of signaling that I was watching them. But they seemed to be enjoying themselves, chatting and giggling as they sipped what looked like two wine coolers.

Thank you, Jenny's girlfriend, I said, *for bringing the alcohol and Jenny's swimsuit.* I hoped it would be just the right combination for loosening the two girls up and taking this spring break adventure to the next level.

After twenty minutes or so of lounging in the tub, the two girls scurried out of the tank and dried themselves off in the kitchen, then headed upstairs to get changed. I followed their movement with the inside cameras, and when they got to my bedroom, I turned on the upstairs audio feed so I could hear what they were saying.

Jenny peeled off her swimsuit then flipped open my nightstand drawer and pointed inside.

"Guess what I discovered last night while I was in Mrs. Jackson's bed?" she said.

Jenny's friend peered into the drawer, then looked up at Jenny with wide eyes.

"Holy shit!" she said. "Are those what I think they are?"

"I can assure you they absolutely are," Jenny smiled.

"But they all look so *different*," her friend said. "I've only seen those gross penis-shaped vibrators. How do these things even *work*?"

Jenny peeled off her swimsuit and jumped on the bed, patting the mattress beside her.

"Why don't you come join me and find out? Some of these devices are really incredible. Don't tell me you've never tried one before."

"Nothing like *that*, that's for sure," her friend said, hesitating.

Jenny reached into the drawer and pulled out the tiny Pocket Rocket vibrator.

"Come on, Niki," she said. "It's just us girls. No one's ever going to know if we have a little extra fun on our sleepover."

"What if Mrs. Jackson's watching on her home security cam?"

Jenny peered down the hallway toward my camera at the top of the stairs, and I quickly turned it so it was facing the other way.

"There's only one camera on each floor, and it can't see in here anyway," Jenny said. "Take your swimsuit off and join me on the bed. We deserve a little break from all our studying."

I heard the sound of clothes dropping to the floor followed by a bed squeaking as her friend joined her on the bed. Then I slowly swiped my finger across the screen, turning the camera back in their direction. Niki was more petite than Jenny, with a typically slender high-school figure. She looked to be about average height and build, but with firm, perky breasts and athletic, toned legs. She sat leaning back against the headboard, with her arms crossed over her chest and her legs extended close together in front of her.

Jenny twisted the base of the Pocket Rocket then handed it to her friend, who ran her fingers over the buzzing end.

"Pretty cool, right?" Jenny said, smiling at Niki, glancing between her legs. "Don't be so bashful. Give it a try."

Niki angled her knees slightly apart and placed the nubby end of the vibrator at the top of her slit, then she suddenly jumped.

"I *know*, right?" Jenny said. "That little thing packs quite a punch, doesn't it?"

"Mmm," Niki nodded, spreading her legs a little further apart.

"You can adjust the intensity of the vibrations by turning the cap on the base of the unit. "I like to ramp it up the more turned on I get."

"How many of these things have you *tried* so far?" Niki said, squirming her hips on the mattress.

"Almost all of them. This is nothing compared to some of the *dual-purpose* vibrators."

"Dual purpose?" Niki said, pinching her eyebrows.

"Most of the other ones stimulate you on the inside and the outside at the same time. You haven't experienced a proper orgasm until you've tried one of these things."

"Why did you give me this *little* one to start with then?" Niki panted, obviously beginning to feel the effects of the targeted stimulation on her clit.

"I didn't want to scare you away too fast," Jenny smiled. "Are you ready to step it up?"

"Definitely," Niki grunted.

"Reach in and take out that pink one that looks like a curled-up snake. I think you're going to like the way it moves inside you."

Niki peered into the drawer and shook her head.

"There's two pink objects that look kind of similar," she said. "Which one?"

"Both," Jenny smiled. "We *both* might be able to get in on the action with this one."

Niki pulled the two objects out of the drawer then Jenny took the smaller piece out of her hand.

"What exactly am I supposed to do with this thing?" Niki said, examining the U-shaped We-Vibe device.

"You slide the fat end inside you with the thinner end pointing up. Then press it all the way up until the connecting part is resting against your opening."

"What are you going to do with the *other* attachment?" Niki said.

"You'll see," Jenny said, flashing her a devilish smile.

Up to this point, I'd just been following the playful banter of the two friends as they tried out the tamer device. But when Niki spread her legs further apart and inserted the thick end of the We-Vibe into her slit, I tore off my pants and reached over for my Lelo vibrator resting on the nightstand. Then I watched Niki press the device deep into her hole until the narrower end rested near the base of her mound.

"This feels kind of weird," Niki said, shaking her head. "How do I turn it on?"

"Leave that up to *me*," Jenny smirked, grasping the remote-control unit and tapping one of the buttons.

"You mean you can–*oh!*" Niki grunted, feeling the internal arm of the We-Vibe unit pulsing against the inside of her pussy.

"Damn straight, girl," Jenny said. "I *told* you Mrs. Jackson has an interesting collection of toys. Let me take the driver's seat while you sit back and enjoy the scenery."

"Mmm," Niki purred, glancing at Jenny's voluptuous tits. "You know I've always fantasized about being with you this way. You have the most amazing body..."

Jenny suddenly leaned over and placed her mouth over one of Niki's tits, sucking her pink teats.

"Oh God, Jenny," Niki panted. "That feels so good..."

"You have *no* idea," Jenny said, flicking her finger over the control knob, activating the clitoral stimulator.

"*Uhnn*," Niki grunted, rolling her hips on the bed as Jenny nibbled her tits and neck. "Fuck me Jenny. Make me come with your hot tongue."

"All in due course, baby," Jenny purred. "I just want you to enjoy this little toy a little longer until you warmed up."

"Oh, I'm getting *warmed up*, alright," Niki groaned, running her fingers through Jenny's hair. "I'm going to cum soon if you keep that up."

"You mean *this*?" Jenny said, flipping the control switch, raising the intensity of the two vibrating arms.

"*Yes!*" Niki panted, thrashing her hips as Jenny suckled on her nubs.

"Oh my God," Niki hissed. "I'm going to come, Jenny. Suck my tits while I cum!"

Suddenly, Niki grabbed the back of Jenny's head with two hands, pulling her face hard against her chest, spreading her legs as far apart as they could go. I zoomed in, watching the vibrator buzzing against her pussy as she slowly lifted her hips off the bed.

"Uhnn!" she groaned, as her orgasm took over her body. "*Oh God, oh God, oh God!*"

Jenny pulled back and peered up at her friend, watching the look of ecstasy wash over her face as she quivered over the bed. When Niki finally dropped her hips back down onto the mattress, Jenny turned the vibrator off and straddled her hips, kissing her passionately.

"*Fuck*, that was hot," she said, nibbling Niki's ear. "I knew you'd enjoy these things."

"Not nearly as much as I like *you*," Niki said, grabbing Jenny's ass and pulling her closer as she pressed her tits against Jenny's breasts. "Can we put away the toys now and just concentrate on touching each other?"

"I thought you'd never ask," Jenny smiled, grinding her pussy against Niki's bare mound.

"I love the feeling of your body up against me," Niki panted. "I want to feel you fucking me *straight up* this time. I'm so wet right now."

"I can tell," Jenny said, sliding her body down Niki's abdomen, pressing her thighs apart until her chest rested against Niki's vulva.

"Rub your tits against me, Jenny," Niki pleaded, squirming her hips against Jenny's mounds.

Jenny raised herself up a few inches and grasped one of her globes with two hands, rubbing it playfully up and down Niki's slit.

Up to this point I'd just been rubbing my Lelo vibrator gently against my opening as I absent-mindedly watched the two girls interact. But when I saw Jenny tit-fucking her friend with her voluptuous breasts, I plunged the G-spot stimulator deep into my pussy, rolling it around as I moaned along with Niki.

"*Fuck*," she groaned. "That feels *way* better than a plastic vibrator. You're so warm and wet."

"You know what *also* feels warmer and wetter than a vibrator?" Jenny said, pushing Niki's knees up toward her chest, then lowering her hips over her friend's splayed pussy. As she placed her ass over Niki's twitching vulva, their pussies touched, and they groaned loudly.

"Jesus," Niki gasped. "Where did you learn to do this? Have you been holding out on me?"

"I've been studying a bit more than just math and chemistry since I've been here," Jenny purred, rolling her hips over Niki's upturned cunny.

"*Holy fuck!*" Niki groaned, feeling Jenny's clit pressing against her own. "This is the hottest thing I've ever done. I never even imagined–"

Jenny leaned forward, engulfing Niki's mouth with her own, pressing her tits against the other girl while the two of them ground their pussies together. I could hear the sexy slurping noises of their wet vulvas sliding over one another as their pink folds spread open for my camera. As they picked up the pace of their rocking motion, they moaned into each other's mouths and Niki wrapped her arms around Jenny's back, digging her fingernails into her skin.

Moments later, they both began squealing as their hips trembled in unison. I zoomed in as far as the camera would go, and just as Niki let out a high-pitched scream, Jenny began squirting all over her friend's perineum as Niki's rosebud puckered in and out. In all my years of watching lesbian trib videos, I'd never seen anything so sexy and raw. As I lay exhausted, drenched in my own pool of cum, I reached over and patted the sheet beside me.

If only you were here with me, I thought, imagining Jenny's body merging with my *own* instead of her friend's. *This trip to paradise isn't be complete without you.*

6

———————

Niki went home the following day and for the rest of my vacation I watched old clips of Jenny playing with my toys. She'd occasionally take out a new one and pleasure herself on my bed or while watching lesbian videos, but I soon longed to be next to her, touching her directly. As I neared the end of my trip, I feared I'd lose her forever once the break was over, so I rescheduled my return flight and came home a day early.

When I got to the front door, I didn't feel comfortable barging in on her unannounced, so I tapped the doorbell. She came to the door wrapped in a large bath towel, and her eyes widened as she paused in the doorway.

"Mrs. Jackson!" she said. "I wasn't expecting you until tomorrow. Is everything okay?"

"Yes," I said, feeling Oscar rubbing himself against the bottom of my leg. "I was just feeling a bit sorry for you having to look after this big house all by yourself. I figured you could use an extra day getting ready to return to school."

"I've been studying hard," Jenny said, "so you needn't have worried. But come in out of the cold–it's your house after all."

"I didn't want to just barge in unannounced. I hope I didn't interrupt you in the middle of anything..."

"Actually, I was just getting ready to take another dip in your pool. It's been such a pleasure enjoying the heated water during the cool evenings."

I smiled, peering at Jenny's hourglass figure in the towel.

"And the hot tub too, I hope. It's a singular pleasure soaking in the stimulating bath when it's cold outside."

"Absolutely," Jenny nodded. "Your place is like a virtual playground for a starved teenager like me."

"Tell you what," I said. "Why don't I drop off my stuff in the bedroom and join you there in a few minutes? I could use another dip in the warm water to ease my transition back to the Chicago weather."

"Sure," Jenny said, noticing my erect nipples in my linen blouse from the chill outside. "Should I get changed?"

"It's starting to get dark, so the neighbors shouldn't be able to spy on us. I don't know about you, but I always enjoy soaking in the hot tub in the raw. It's just us girls, after all."

"I agree," Jenny smiled. "I'll meet you there in a few minutes."

I rushed upstairs and tore off my clothes, then threw on a robe and headed downstairs. When I opened the door to the veranda, Jenny had already submerged herself in the tub, and she peered up at me with dripping hair.

"You certainly look like you've made yourself at home," I smiled, dropping my robe and stepping into the swirling water a few feet away from her.

"It's been kind of fun, actually," she said. "I almost don't want to go back home. I could get used to hanging around here a little longer."

My heart skipped a beat, wondering if I should ask her to stay another night.

"Did you have any trouble operating any of the equipment?" I said, making a veiled reference to my sex toy collection. "Has everything been okay with the pool, the car, and other devices?"

"Yes," Jenny smiled. "Good on all fronts. Were you able to check in periodically to make sure I wasn't burning your house down?"

"Once in a while," I said. "I didn't want to interfere with your privacy too much. Mostly just to check that you were safe and well stocked up."

"I've been able to keep everything replenished pretty well," Jenny nodded. "Thanks to the use of your car. Thanks again for letting me have the use it."

"My pleasure," I said. "Have you been able to get out and see many of your friends while I was away?"

"Not too much," Jenny said. "I had a friend come over for a sleepover one night to help break up the monotony."

"Did you show her around and avail yourselves of all the amenities?" I said, resisting the temptation to let her know just how much I knew she'd enjoyed that sleepover.

"Yes," Jenny blinked. "We went for a swim, had a relaxing hot tub–"

"Did you discover the special *nozzle*?" I smiled.

"You mean–"

"The one that sprays in a particularly delightful place."

"It was hard *not* to," Jenny blushed. "Once you find the right spot, you don't exactly want to move."

"And your *friend*? Did she discover it too?"

"Yes, but I think she was a bit self-conscious about trying it in my presence. I think that's something meant to be enjoyed more by yourself..."

"I don't know about *that*," I said, shifting my body over in front of the spigot. "I kind of missed this while I was away. Do you mind–?"

"Not at all," Jenny smiled. "After all, it's just us girls, right?"

"Right," I said, spreading my legs apart and shifting my weight forward to direct the spray onto my buzzing clit. "Mmm, yes–this is one luxury they didn't have at my expensive resort in Bora Bora."

"It must have been fun though," Jenny said, watching the expression on my face as I squirmed under the water. "There must have been lots of other exciting things to do there."

"I guess so," I said, catching my breath. "Snorkeling, sailing, swimming in the lagoon. It gets pretty old though when you're by yourself. I found myself checking in with you just to keep myself company."

"I hope you didn't catch me skinny dipping in your pool."

"I did indeed," I panted. "And in the hot tub. It looked like you were enjoying yourself as much as I am right now."

"I thought *maybe* you were watching me," Jenny said. "I caught the cameras pointed in my direction a few times."

"Did you *like* being watched?" I said.

"Sometimes," Jenny said. "It was kind of *stimulating* to be honest, knowing you were catching me occasionally without any clothes on."

"Oh yes," I groaned. "I caught you more than once."

"Did you enjoy watching me as much as I liked the idea of you watching me?" Jenny said, lifting an eyebrow.

"You have no idea," I panted. "Almost as much as I am right now."

"Mmm," Jenny said, dipping her hands below the surface of the water and shifting her weight on the seat opposite me. "I wish I could have spied on *you* as much as you were with me. You know, I always kind of had a thing for you, even when I was little. I always thought you were the most beautiful woman I'd ever seen."

"Oh my God, Jenny," I said, getting even more turned on knowing she found me attractive. "You've blossomed into the most beautiful, sexy young adult. *You're* the one I've had a crush on since you came over to my place."

"Oh Mrs. Jackson," Jenny panted, her cheeks beginning to flush.

"I think it's time you started calling me Jade," I smiled. "Seeing as how we're both stimulating ourselves under the water while watching each other."

"Jade," Jenny purred. "You have no idea how often I've fantasized about you."

"I must have come a hundred times thinking about you while I was away," I said. "I've wanted to feel your body against mine practically from the moment I left."

"Yes," Jenny moaned. "You're going to make me cum watching you."

"Yes, baby," I hissed. "Let it go. I'm almost there too."

"Uhnn," Jenny groaned, spreading her mouth wide open as she looked at me with glazed eyes.

Suddenly, I felt a bolt of electricity running through me as my orgasm washed over me. While we jerked and moaned together in simultaneous climax under the swirling water, we couldn't take our eyes off each other.

"Oh my God," Jenny panted after we both calmed down. "That was *so* hot."

"Let's get the hell out of here and go upstairs where we can do this *properly*," I said. "I need to feel a *warm body* next to me, not just an artificial water jet."

"I was thinking exactly the same thing," Jenny smiled.

The two of us scampered out of the hot tub and ran upstairs, giggling like two girls. When we got to the bed, I didn't even bother to pull down the covers, pulling her onto the mattress with me and entangling our legs together. It was electrifying feeling her naked body rubbing against mine, and for the longest time I was content to rub our slippery bodies together while we kissed passionately. The feeling of Jenny's big tits pressing against mine was sublime, and I was in no hurry to get down to more serious business.

But after a while, I felt Jenny's hands roaming lower on my body, and when her hand slipped into the cleft under my ass, I pulled back and looked at her.

"Jenny," I panted. "You have no idea how much I've wanted to feel your touch on my body.

"And yours on mine," Jenny grinned.

When she slipped two fingers into my hole, I squeezed her tits with two hands, pinching her large teats with my fingers.

"Uhnn," I groaned, feeling my juices spreading all over her hand. "I want to fuck you so bad."

"Yes please," Jenny said.

I pulled her hand out of my pussy, then pushed her down onto the bed and straddled her crotch with my thighs on either side of her hips.

"Does this position look familiar?" I said.

Jenny's eyes widened as she peered up at me with a look of shock.

"*No way!* You weren't watching me and my girlfriend when we were in your bedroom?!"

"I hope you don't mind," I nodded. "You did leave the door open just enough for my camera to zoom in from down the hallway."

"I was kind of hoping you were," Jenny smiled. "Did you see us playing with your toys too?"

"Absolutely," I grinned. "Your girlfriend is almost as hot as you are."

"Maybe the three of us can try this sometime," Jenny said. "I think she's become attracted to girls as much as I have since I've been here."

"Maybe another time," I said. "Right now, I just want to look at your magnificent body while I fuck you with my pussy."

"Yes, Jade," Jenny purred. "Fuck me with your pussy. I want to feel you cumming against me this time."

I rolled Jenny onto her side, pulling her right leg up onto my chest, then I tilted my hips forward until our pussies touched.

"Oh God," Jenny gasped. "Your pussy feels so hot."

"As hot as your *girlfriend's*?"

"It's *different* with you," she said. "I've never–"

"Been on the bottom before?" I smiled.

"Not like this," she said. "I *like* being fucked by you."

As I mashed my pussy into hers, I heard the familiar sloshing sound of our wet vulvas sucking and caressing each other's lips. I grabbed her tits with my two hands and squeezed them as hard as I could, feeling my ass slide over her slick thigh as we rocked our hips together.

"Jade," Jenny growled, peering at me with wild eyes. "I'm going to cum. Oh God, I'm going to cum all over your hot pussy."

Suddenly, I felt her hips shaking underneath me as a sexy flush rolled over her face.

"Yes, Jenny," I panted. "You're so beautiful. I'm going to cum with you, baby. Oh *fuck*–"

I pulled Jenny's upturned leg hard against my chest, feeling my pussy beginning to pulse in powerful contractions. Unable to hold it any longer, I gushed all over her slit as we wailed in delirious union. After what seemed like an eternity shaking and looking into each other's eyes while we enjoyed a long climax together, I collapsed onto the bed beside her and stroked her pretty face with the back of my hand.

"That was incredible," Jenny panted. "I don't think I've cum that hard in my whole life."

"Not even with my *Rabbit* vibrator or that funny finger-shaped sex toy?"

"Those were pretty good, I have to admit," she smiled. "But nothing like feeling your body next to mine." She looked between our legs at the huge wet spot that had formed on top of the comforter. "Plus, you've got a *special* power that none of those other devices have. That was the most stimulating shower I've had in a long time."

"There's more where that came from," I said, grinning like a Cheshire Cat. "Are you ready to try this again in a more equally yoked position?"

"Yes, but how would that work exactly?" Jenny asked. "Doesn't one of us kind of have to take the lead role when we're connected that way?"

I reached over and swung open my nightstand drawer, pulling out the long double-sided pink dildo.

"Not if something *else* is connecting us together," I smiled. "Have you had a chance to try *this* one yet?"

"I was kind of saving that one for you," Jenny said. "I figured you'd be able to show me how to use it properly."

"You got that right, girl," I smirked. "Now get up on all fours while I fuck you from behind with this thing."

"I like the sound of that," Jenny purred.

As I pressed one end of the dildo into my sopping hole and pressed my ass backwards towards hers, I tilted my head down and peered between my legs at her swinging tits.

This was one holiday I'd never soon forget, I thought to myself.

VICTORIA RUSH

THE
HAIR
SALON

LESBIAN EROTICA

1

___

I never particularly enjoyed having my hair colored professionally. Besides the painstakingly long process of having my strands individually dyed and wrapped in ugly foils, I had to sit in an uncomfortable chair for two hours smelling the awful stench of the coloring chemicals. At least I had my phone to keep me distracted for part of the time, but there's only so many games of Candy Crush you can play before you literally feel like pulling your hair out.

After my last treatment, I'd sworn off the idea of having it ever done again, but after seeing one of my favorite actresses at a televised awards ceremony in a pretty sun-bleached bob, I decided to give it one more try. I googled her red carpet photo, then took a screenshot on my phone and scheduled an appointment with my colorist. On the day of my appointment, the salon was busier than usual and I scrunched up my nose smelling the reek of chemicals permeating the room as three other women sat patiently in their chairs waiting for their color to set.

"Good morning, Jade," the salon owner Nikki said greeting me, motioning for me to take the last open chair when she finished with her last client. "It's been a while since you've been in for a coloring. What's the occasion?"

"Nothing special," I said, tapping my phone to pull up the photo I'd saved. "I just thought this new look Amanda Seyfried was sporting at the Golden Globes looked pretty glam, and I felt like a change."

"Mmm," Nikki said, nodding her head as she peered at my screen. "I also noticed her on the show last week. It's a spectacular cut, and that strawberry blonde color looks great on her."

"Do you think you can duplicate it?"

"Of course, but are you sure about the color? You've been a straight blonde for quite a while now, and I know how much you dislike the coloring process. It'll be difficult to match your natural color again without letting it grow out."

"What the hell," I said, looking at all the other women tied up in hair clips while they stared at their smartphones. "You only live once, right? No pain, no gain."

"That's *one* way of putting it," Nikki chuckled. "I'll try to make this as painless as possible. Hold tight while I mix the color for you. Can I borrow your phone to use the photo as a benchmark?"

"Of course," I said, giving her a wink as I handed over my phone. "Just don't drop it. The cost to replace it is even higher than your coloring fees."

"Not to worry," she chuckled. "I'm pretty sure my prices are lower than what Amanda Seyfried paid for her do."

While Nikki retreated to the rear of the store to prepare the treatment, I looked at the panel of mirrors lining the wall, scanning the faces of the other women getting their hair colored. Each of them looked bored out of their minds while they tapped their phone screens as they shifted uncomfortably in their salon chairs. When one of them looked up to catch my gaze, I smiled at her with a lopsided grin to convey my sympathy with her predicament.

Color? she mouthed the word, pointing to the mess atop her head.

I nodded and she shook her head with a frown, knowing what I was in for.

A few minutes later, Nikki returned, placing her mixing bowl and brushes on the table beside my chair.

"All set?" she said, peering at me in the mirror.

"As ready as I'll ever be," I said, gripping the armrests on my chair tightly.

"What *is* it about this process that you abhor so much, anyway?" she said, noticing my white knuckles.

"You mean besides the awful stench of the chemicals and having to stare at my ugly head all tied up in greasy knots and tangled hair clips for two hours?" I scoffed. "Nothing gives me more pleasure."

"Well, you don't exactly have to stare at *yourself* the whole time," she said, handing my phone back to me. "Surely you can find some *other* things to keep yourself amused while connected to our salon Wi-Fi. Maybe you can watch a movie of your favorite actress or search for your next hair style."

"Maybe," I said, shifting uncomfortably in the upright chair. "But I already spend way too much time staring at my computer screen all day long. It would be nice to have a *different* kind of distraction when I get out of the house."

"You mean besides the stimulating conversation with your favorite stylist?"

"You know how much I love getting caught up with you, Nikki," I smiled. "But getting my hair dyed isn't quite the same as getting it cut. After you put the color in, I'm pretty much left to my own devices for an hour and a half while you look after other clients."

"It's the nature of the beast," she nodded. "It takes that long for the dye to permeate your hair and properly set. I hazard to say that Amanda Seyfried had to sit in her salon's studio for more than two hours to create her new look."

"I know," I said, shaking my head apologetically. "The end result is normally worth the investment. It's just that the *rest* of the salon experience is actually quite stimulating and enjoyable. The shampoo and head massage you give me afterwards is practically worth the price of admission alone. It's too bad you couldn't find something equally enjoyable to keep me occupied the rest of the time."

"What did you have in mind?" Nikki said as she began to separate my hair with her comb and brush in the color paste. "I enjoy your head massage almost as much as you do, but if you wanted me to give you a *full-body* massage the entire time it takes for your color to set, I'd have to triple my rates to cover the overhead."

I paused, peering at Nikki in the mirror with a sly smile.

"Maybe you could find some *other* kind of way to massage me while you're busy tending to other clients' needs," I smiled. "With all the advances in modern technology, it shouldn't be too hard to upgrade this chair with some new enhancements..."

"Like one of those expensive massage chairs?" she said.

"I was thinking more like a *Sybian* massage chair," I grinned. "To stimulate some *other* parts of my body. That could definitely keep me amused for a little while."

"No way," Nikki said, suddenly cocking her head toward me in the mirror. "Are you *serious*? Right here in the *open*, in full display of the other customers?"

"It's not like they'd know any better," I smirked. "With me covered in a long apron and all the other buzz of activity going on in the salon, they probably wouldn't even hear the sound of the vibrator."

Nikki paused for a moment while she looked at me in the mirror.

"You could always bring one of your *own* if you needed that kind of distraction."

"Possibly," I said. "But I'd still have to sneak it out of my purse and position it under my gown to hold it steady. It would be a lot more convenient if you had something built in to the chair that I could control from the armrests."

"You're actually serious about this, aren't you?" Nikki said, staring at me incredulously.

"Why not? Think about the competitive edge it could give you. It wouldn't take long for your place to become known not only for its cutting-edge hair styles, but also for its invigorating salon experience."

"That's assuming we don't get raided by the cops first for running an illicit massage parlor–"

"Except that *you* wouldn't be actually doing the massage," I said. "It would all be self-administered from the privacy of our own chairs, at our own discretion."

"What about the *rest* of my clientele?" Nikki said, still not convinced. "I'm not sure some of the older women would approve of such licentious activity..."

"You never know until you try," I smiled. "I'm guessing some of them might appreciate it more than you imagine. Besides, you don't have to tell everybody about the special features."

"Where do you come up with these crazy ideas?" she said, shaking her head.

"Remember I was telling you the last time I was in here about some of the amazing new sex toys coming onto the market? The only difference in this case is that your clientele would be enjoying them in a completely different setting."

"In full view of all the other customers?"

"They don't need to know what's going on in the privacy of someone else's chair. But if they *did*, that might only increase the excitement level all the more."

"Jesus, Jade," Nikki said, wrinkling her forehead. "I don't know..."

"Why don't you outfit *one* chair to start? And only tell your most trusting clients. If they object to the idea, you can always remove the feature. But I have a feeling this might up your game and dramatically increase your book of business. You might even be able to raise your already exorbitant fees."

"You have a wicked mind, you know that, right?" Nikki said, peering at me in the mirror with a raised eyebrow.

"So are you thinking of giving it a try?" I smirked.

"You've certainly piqued my interest," she smiled, rubbing her thighs together while she finished setting the foils in my hair. "If nothing else, I'll be able to use the chair to keep *myself* amused when things get quiet in the salon..."

2

After my hair coloring finished, I decided to forego the styling portion of my appointment, hoping Nikki would take my suggestion to heart and make some modifications before my next session. When I visited the studio two weeks later, my panties were already wet in anticipation of trying out the new upgrades.

"Hey beautiful," she said when I entered the salon. "Love your new color. Do you miss being a blonde?"

"I'm not feeling quite as *stupid*, that's for sure," I grinned.

"*Good* one," Nikki laughed. "But you can't fool me. I know all the brilliant ideas rolling around in that pretty head of yours, no matter how well you try to camouflage it."

"Speaking of, have you made any changes to your setup based on my suggestions?"

"Let's talk about it over by the sink," Nikki nodded. "Maybe I can get you warmed up with a nice wash and head massage."

"You're twisting my arm," I said. "You know that's the favorite part of my visit."

"Maybe not for much longer," she smiled, leading me to the back of the studio toward the bank of sinks on the far wall.

"So?" I said, sitting in the chair opposite one of the sinks and tilting my head back into the curved depression to rest my neck. "I'm dying to know if you've made any upgrades!"

"*Possibly,*" Nikki teased, adjusting the water temperature and pointing the warm spray over my head. "You'll just have to wait until you get seated for your cut."

"Who needs a vibrating chair when I've got the next best thing standing right over top of me?" I purred, feeling the soft wash flowing over my scalp as Nikki massaged the shampoo into my hair.

"Oh?" she smiled, kneading my head firmly with the tips of her fingers. "You like to be *fingered* once in a while instead?"

"If it's by someone as pretty and sexy as you, absolutely."

"Maybe I should expand my repertoire by offering full-body washes to my customers as well?" she smirked.

"Don't get me started," I groaned, rolling my hips at the thought of Nikki directing the pulsating spray on my wet pussy. "I'm already worked up enough at the thought of you watching me getting stimulated while you do my hair."

"I have to admit, it's gotten *me* pretty damn excited at the thought also. I can't wait to give this thing a try."

"You mean I'll be the first?"

"If you don't count me," she smiled. "I mean I had to test it before offering it to my customers, right?"

"And?" I said, batting my eyelashes as the warm spray spilled down over my forehead. "Does it work?"

"If you consider three incredibly powerful orgasms in the space of ten minutes a success, then I suppose so."

"*Fuck*, Nikki," I panted. "You're going to get me off right here if you keep talking like that."

"Judging by the spreading wet spot in your jeans, it would appear so," she said, glancing at my crotch. "We better get you gowned up before somebody guesses what's going on."

"Ok, but can I take a rain check on the full-body wash? I've been fantasizing about getting you alone for myself since the first day I stepped foot in your salon."

"That can be arranged," Nikki smiled. "I have to admit I was thinking of *you* too while I was trying out the new chair."

"*Damn*, girl," I grunted while she rinsed off the last of the shampoo residue from my head. "Clean me up, I can't wait to try this out!"

Nikki tilted my head up over the sink then draped a dry towel over my head, rubbing my hair vigorously while she tossed my head from side to side.

"Holy shit," I said, leaning forward and panting as she removed the towel and held out her hand to help me up from the chair. "Talk about *rubbing* one out. Nobody quite gives head like you do, Nikki."

"I'll take that as a compliment," she said, leading me over to the styling chair furthest from the front window.

When I approached the chair, I noticed a small triangle-shaped bump in the middle of the seat and four new buttons embedded in the right armrest. One was colored green and another red, with the other two simply marked 'Up' and 'Down'.

"This looks interesting," I said, rolling my fingers over the bulge. "It's a little different than the *Sybian* chair I'm used to, but it looks promising."

"Well, I couldn't very well place a four-inch-long dildo in the middle of my chair without making it obvious what it was there for."

"How are you going to explain this slightly less obtrusive addition?"

"If anyone asks, I'll just tell them it's meant to show where they're supposed to sit and not move around while I'm cutting their hair. But something tells me there won't be too many complaints once they figure out what it's *really* there for."

"Strap me in, babe," I smiled. "I'm ready to take it for the first test ride."

I climbed onto the chair then spread my legs while pressing my hips forward until I felt the leading edge of the bump pushing into my slit.

"Very ingenious," I nodded approvingly. "The shape conforms perfectly with the Vee of my vulva."

"I thought it would provide more surface area to stimulate your entire crotch area," Nikki nodded, throwing a plastic gown over my chest and tying it gently behind my neck.

"Brilliant," I said, already feeling my clit starting to tingle as I humped the tip with my hips. "Who did you get to set this up? It almost looks like a factory install."

"One of my clients has an electronics background. I took a couple of hours to install the equipment and re-thread the upholstery to hide the internal wiring. But it turned out better than I expected."

"So I'm not *really* the first one to give this a try then?" I grinned, peering at her with a raised eyebrow.

"You'll be the first one to try it in *public*," Nikki smiled.

"How does it work exactly?" I said, brushing my fingers over the controls.

"I wanted to make it as simple as possible to use," she said. "The green button turns the vibrator on and the red one turns it off. The other two buttons control the intensity of the unit, up and down."

"No controls for setting different *pulse* patterns?"

"This isn't exactly a state-of-the-art sex toy shop," she said. "But I have a feeling you'll find the basic controls more than adequate. Fire it up to give it a try."

I pressed the green button with my index finger then held my thumb down over the Up button for a few seconds, feeling the triangle-shaped hump beginning to vibrate between my legs.

"*Still* think you need multiple modes of operation to make it work?" Nikki smiled, noticing me jerk suddenly in the chair.

"Um..." I grunted, toggling the vibrator speed up a few notches. "I think this will do just fine."

"I *thought* you might like it," Nikki said, running her hands through my mane as she began to trim it with her scissors. "Do you think you'll be able to stay still while I cut your hair? I wouldn't want to poke an eye out or something while you're busy stimulating yourself."

"Or make me look like *Edward Scissorhands* by the time you're finished," I chuckled, feeling the pleasure beginning to spread around my hips.

"Exactly."

As Nikki began to style my hair, I closed my eyes, pressing my vulva harder against the bump in the chair. The harder I pushed against it, the further it pressed the seam of my jeans into my slit, heightening my pleasure even more.

"*Fuck*, Nikki," I panted. "This thing is perfectly designed to hit all the right places. I only wish I could enjoy it *naked* to experience its full potential."

"You might want to come with a skirt and no panties next time," she said, cocking her head. "It's a million times better in the raw."

"I bet it is," I said, beginning to roll my hips under my apron. "But it still feels fucking awesome even with all my clothes on."

"Good enough to elevate my already exorbitant fees?" Nikki smiled.

"I'd pay *twice* your fee to sit in this thing for forty-five minutes while you do my hair. Something tells me you're about to become the most popular hair salon in town."

"We'll have to see about that," Nikki said. "I'm just happy to see my clients walking out of the place with a big grin on their faces."

"Ugnnn," I groaned, feeling the familiar pangs of a climax building up inside me. "Oh God, Nikki..."

"Let it go, baby," she purred, staring back at me in the mirror. "Let me watch you come while I hold your head. You've got a lovely red flush to match your new strawberry highlights."

As I stared back at Nikki feeling my pleasure rapidly rising, my mouth began to part and my eyes glazed over as I felt my orgasm washed over me. Trying not to reveal the pleasure I was feeling to the patrons on the other chairs beside me, I gripped the chair armrests tightly, trying to hold myself still while my body convulsed in powerful contractions.

"Damn, girl," Nikki purred, listening to me panting next to her while my head bobbed softly in her hands. "That's fucking hot. I nearly came *with* you watching you. This might be harder than I expected trying to concentrate on cutting your hair while you're enjoying yourself."

"This is *insane!*" I said, trying to catch my breath as my body jerked softly coming down from my climax. "There's something about doing this in full view of your other customers without them knowing what's going on that takes it to a whole new level."

"That, and not being able to squeal while you're coming under your apron?" Nikki smiled.

"Yeah," I nodded. "It reminds me of a dinner party I attended a while back where everybody watched me getting off while someone caressed me under the table. But in this case, it's even more stimulating trying to *hide* my pleasure."

"Don't let me stop you now," Nikki grinned. "I still need another twenty minutes or so to finish your cut. Knock yourself out while we continue pretending like nothing special is happening. You haven't even tried the maximum speed setting yet."

"I want to make it last," I said, turning the vibrator speed back down to build up to another climax. "You don't want me jumping out of my seat before you're finished, do you?"

"Go for it," she said. "I'm interested to see just how much you can stand while sitting still."

"You're on," I smiled, holding my finger over the Up button as the vibrator began to buzz harder against my clit.

"Mhhh," I grunted, pressing my cunt harder against the pointy bump. "I hope you've got plenty of disinfectant left over when I'm finished. Cause I'm pretty sure I'm going to leave a big wet spot on your chair by the time this is over."

"I hope so," Nikki said, smiling at me in the mirror as my face began to twist and distort trying to mask my rising pleasure. "You might not be the *only* one needing to wear a skirt to your next hair appointment. This is turning me on so much watching you, I'm generating my *own* wet spot."

"Mmm," I groaned, gazing into Nikki's eyes as she peered back at me in the mirror. "I'm imagining it's your wet pussy rubbing up against me right now instead of this leather vibrator. I can't wait to get you into bed with your clothes off."

"Or under my sink?"

"However I can get you," I grunted while turning the vibrator speed up to the maximum setting. "I just want to feel your sexy body pressed up against me."

As I began to growl with a soft animal sound, some of the other women flanking me turned their heads to watch me in the mirror.

"You better keep your emotions in check lest you frighten the rest of my customers away," Nikki said, noticing the distraction of the other customers.

"I'm trying," I panted while gyrating my hips more rapidly under the fluttering apron. "But I don't think there's any turning back now."

"Damn, Jade," Nikki hissed over my shoulder. "This has to be the sexiest thing I've ever seen. I had no idea this would be so enjoyable for the *rest* of us when you proposed this idea."

"Maybe you should be giving me a *discount* instead of charging a premium?" I smiled, noticing the flush in my cheeks spreading down my neck as I bit my lip trying to suppress my rising pleasure.

"Maybe," Nikki panted beside me as she squeezed her legs together trying to stimulate her own aching clit. "This is sure better than any sexy movie or porn site I've ever watched."

"Oh Nikki," I grunted, gaping my mouth open as I approached another powerful climax.

"Yes, Jade," she groaned with her own sex flush beginning to roll over her cheeks. "You're going to make me come just watching you..."

"Oh *fuckkkk*," I hissed as another orgasm washed over me while I began twitching and convulsing in my chair, gripping the armrests with white knuckles trying to hold myself steady.

By now, everybody in the room was staring at me squirming and moaning in my chair as the powerful vibrator between my legs continued to oscillate against my convulsing pussy. By the time my minute-long orgasm subsided, the only sound that could be heard in the room was the soft buzzing of the vibrator between my legs. While

Nikki continued to cut my hair like nothing unusual was happening, another client sat in the salon chair next to me.

"What kind of cut would you like to today?" her stylist said to the woman.

"I'll have what *she's* having," the girl said, smiling at my flushed face.

3

———————

After my previous visit to the hair salon, I could hardly wait for my next appointment. But this time, I came fully prepared, wearing a short skirt and no panties. I didn't want anything coming between me and the pointy vibrator embedded in Nikki's salon chair. When I entered the studio, she greeted me warmly at the front door, kissing me on both cheeks.

"You scheduled earlier than usual," she said.

"I was just getting itchy for another treatment," I smiled. "Ever since my last visit, I've been tingling all over awaiting another turn in your special chair."

"I see you came properly *prepared* this time," she said, peering at my high skirt. "Were you looking for a *coloring* or a cut? We usually recommend at least six weeks between dye treatments."

"Just a little trim will be fine this time," I said. "That should be more than enough time to satisfy my craving."

"Mmm," Nikki smiled. "I think we can get that looked after. Shall we start with the usual preliminaries?"

"Absolutely," I said. "I can't think of any better foreplay than another head massage from my favorite stylist."

Nikki led me to the bank of sinks on the back wall, and I assumed the wash position, tilting my head back as I spread my legs apart.

"So, what's been the response to your expanded suite of services?" I said, peering up at her while she adjusted the water temperature.

"Better than I expected. In fact, I've had to outfit the rest of the chairs based on unprecedented demand."

"Oh?" I said. "Your customers seem to be *enjoying* the upgrades?"

"That's a bit of an understatement," Nikki said, motioning toward the line of salon chairs filled with women. "I've never seen the place as busy as it's been these past few weeks."

"You don't think it's because of your reputation for superb hair styling?" I grinned.

"I'm pretty sure it's because of something *else*," she smiled, rubbing my head vigorously while she peered down at my skirt hiking up my bare thighs. "In fact, today's appointment is on me. If this keeps up, I might have to give you a free lifetime membership."

"Don't sweat it, babe," I moaned, enjoying her wet rub-down. I'm willing to pay your regular rate just to experience this exquisite head massage."

"I've made some new upgrades," Nikki smiled. "I have a feeling you're going to enjoy your *next* massage even more."

"Do tell," I said, flipping up my skirt to reveal my glistening pussy. "You're making me wet in a few *other* places imagining what enhancements you've made."

"I've been trying out a different kind of vibrator on one of the chairs. It's been in especially high demand since I had it installed. Unfortunately, it's booked up solid for three weeks, so you'll have to wait until your next visit to give it a try. But I can guarantee it'll be worth the wait."

"You've still got the regular vibrator installed on the other chairs?"

"Not to worry," she smiled, rinsing off the last of the shampoo residue into the sink. "You'll still be able to keep yourself properly amused while I cut your hair. Although you might find it even *more* interesting watching the reaction of the some of the other customers in the newly outfitted chairs."

"You've got that right," I said, peering over at the lineup of attractive women facing the mirror. "Nothing excites me more than watching a pretty girl get off, especially while she's stimulating herself."

"Well then, I've got a treat for you today. You'll be sitting in the chair next to the newly upgraded one. If you can't experience it directly, at least you can enjoy the next best thing."

Nikki led me over to the same chair I used last time, but before I sat down, I glanced at the empty seat next to me, noticing some new controls on the armrest and a strange slit in the middle of the fabric.

"What happened to the vibrator on the other chair?" I said.

"Oh it's still there," Nikki smiled. "It's just hiding out of sight beneath the upholstery. This one's got a new animated feature that lends an entirely new definition to the idea of yoni massage."

"You mean...?"

"Exactly," Nikki nodded. "I decided to take a page out of your Sybian playbook to elevate this massage experience to a whole new level."

"No fair!" I protested. "If you'd told me about that, I'd have waited a couple of extra weeks for my next appointment!"

"Who are you kidding?" Nikki smirked, throwing a gown over me while I hiked up my skirt and positioned my pussy over the triangle-shaped bulge. "I know you too well to know that you wouldn't be able to hold off any longer than absolutely necessary to get back into this seat. And neither could I. I've been fantasizing about watching you squirming in my chair ever since your last visit."

I turned my head, noticing a pretty brunette taking a seat in the chair next to me while her colorist prepared the treatment materials.

"Let's get this party started," I smiled. "I'm dying to take this thing for another ride."

As Nikki started to style my hair, I watched the pretty girl next to me making small talk with her colorist as she brushed in the dye. The girl hadn't placed her fingers on the armrest controls yet, and for a few minutes I wondered if she was even aware of the newly installed feature.

"What are you waiting for?" Nikki said, noticing me staring at the girl.

"Oh," I said, peering back up at her. "I was just wondering if you've told *all* of your customers about the new features."

"We didn't *have* to," she grinned. "Word got around pretty fast. We lost a few customers who were initially put off by the idea, but we more than made up for it with a rush of new customers who flocked to our studio to try it out. I think it's fair to say that *all* of our clients know about our expanded services at this point."

"And willing to try them *out*?" I said, peering at the new buttons on the adjacent chair.

"Take a look at the faces of the other women lining the wall. Do you notice anything different?"

I peered into the mirror, scanning the bank of chairs occupied by the other women whose hair was tied up in hair clips and coloring foil. Some of them had their eyes closed while they shifted quietly in their chairs, while others smiled at one another as their heads bobbed gently atop their shoulders. But virtually all of them had a flush on their faces as they panted softly. Everyone except the pretty brunette seated next to me, who still seemed preoccupied chatting with her colorist.

"Hmm," I nodded. "They don't look nearly as bored as usual. But not everybody seems to be enjoying themselves equally. Are you sure all of the chairs are outfitted the same way?"

"All but the one next to you. It's just that not everybody likes to take advantage of the feature while they're engaged with their stylist. Some prefer to enjoy the experience when they have a little more privacy."

"If you can call being lined up cheek-by-jowl in front of a salon-wide mirror *private*," I chuckled.

"At least they're all covered in a cape and nobody can see what's going on underneath it. Nobody knows for sure exactly who's doing what at any given time."

"Although it's not too hard to tell where each of them are in their arousal cycle," I grinned, watching one of the women at the far end parting her mouth as the flush on her face began to spread down her neck.

"It's pretty hard to hide it once you get to a certain point," Nikki nodded. "But most of the girls keep the vibration setting at a low level most of the time. You can only take the full intensity of the vibrator for so long."

"True," I said, watching another woman beginning to jerk spastically in her chair as she slipped over the edge. "But that doesn't stop some of us from adjusting the levels to experience *multiple* orgasms depending on how long we have to sit in the chair."

"You mean like you did *last* time?" Nikki smiled.

"I had a little help watching *you* getting just as turned on watching me."

"I did," Nikki smiled. "But it's not quite the same as receiving direct stimulation to the targeted area."

"Speaking of..." I murmured, glancing over at the girl seated next to me. "Do you think we're going to see the pretty brunette getting a little workout before we're finished?"

"Give it a few more minutes," Nikki said, nodding toward the colorist as she picked up her materials to let the dye set. "This one's a little shy."

After her stylist left to look after other clients, the girl darted her eyes across the mirror and I glanced away so as not to make her feel scrutinized. Soon after, her hand wandered over her armrest controls and she groaned, sinking lower in her chair. Before long, her hips began to move rhythmically under her gown and her breathing beginning to escalate.

"What exactly did you *put* in that chair?" I whispered to Nikki, trying to keep my lips still so the girl didn't suspect I was spying on her.

"You'll just have to wait until your next visit to find out," Nikki smiled. "That is, if you remember to schedule your appointment before it's booked solid for another month.

"Nnngh," the girl began to moan as she closed her eyes, gripping her armrests more tightly with both hands.

"*Jesus,*" I said, beginning to feel my juices pooling between my thighs.

I'd been so distracted watching the girl next to me, I hadn't even bothered to turn on my vibrator. I flicked the on switch and pressed my hips forward while I ramped up the speed, feeling the pointy tip sinking deep between my folds.

"Whatever it is," I panted, "it seems to be exciting her even more than mine. If there's such a thing as reincarnation, I want to come back as that salon chair."

"She's pretty fucking hot, that's for sure," Nikki chuckled next to me. "Enjoy it, baby. At least *one* of us will be able to get off watching the show."

As a deep flush began to roll over her face, the girl grunted more loudly while her apron fluttered rapidly from the action of her writhing hips.

"*Uh–uh-uh,*" she groaned, squeezing her eyelids tighter.

"*Fuck me,*" I grunted, becoming increasingly turned on watching her inch closer toward an orgasm.

"Soon enough, babe," Nikki purred, rubbing her mound against the side of my chair as she watched the girl's rising pleasure along with me. "You have no idea what you're in for next time."

I held my finger over the Up button on my armrest, adjusting the vibrator to its maximum speed while I moaned in tandem with the girl next to me. Just as I started to feel my own orgasm welling up inside me, she suddenly flung her eyelids open, staring at me in the mirror with wide eyes.

"Oh my God," she groaned, jerking her torso forcefully as her climax took hold of her.

"Fuckkk," I groaned with my own orgasm washing over me while we stared at each other twitching in our chairs.

Suddenly the entire room was filled with the sound of the rest of the women moaning and gasping while they all stared at the two of us cumming hard in our chairs. The pretty brunette never took her eyes off me as we gaped our mouths open together in mutual plea-sure. Even Nikki grunted noisily beside me while she held onto the side of my chair for support as she ground her pussy into my armrest.

"Holy *fuck*," I muttered after we came down from our powerful climaxes. "I have *got* to try that thing out as soon as it's available. Preferably while it's still covered with that beauty's juices."

"I'll see if I can schedule it before you leave," Nikki smiled, straightening herself up trying to concentrate on finishing my hair.

4

———————

The three weeks I had to wait for my next hair appointment couldn't pass by fast enough while I fantasized about trying out Nikki's newly upgraded salon chair. All I could think about was the pretty brunette twisting and squirming in her seat while she gripped her armrests with bear claws. Whatever Nikki had installed under her seat had caused her to have an incredibly strong orgasm while she convulsed in her chair for almost a full minute. When I entered the studio, my pussy was already dripping wet in anticipation as I tried to hide the rivers of juices running down the inside of my thighs under my short skirt.

"Hey beautiful," Nikki said, kissing me on my cheek as she pressed her breasts against mine in a tight hug. "Are you ready to try out my new chair this time?"

"Are you *kidding* me," I said, pulling her hand over my ass cheeks to feel my slick thighs. "I haven't been this wet since my first lesbian experience."

"Well, you're about to have an entirely *new* kind of girl-on-girl experience this time," she said.

"You mean while you rub me down under the sink?" I smiled.

"Well that's not exactly *new*, but with you already this worked up, maybe you'll enjoy it even more this time."

"*Do* me," I panted into her ear. "I want to feel you finger me until I squeal like a baby."

"You might get a bit lucky," she said, leading me by the hand to the back of the room. "We've got the sinks all to *ourselves* since the rest of my clients have been already prepped."

I lay my head in the depression in one of the sinks, and Nikki wasted no time spraying the pulsating water over my scalp as she lathered in the shampoo while I stared up at her.

"That feels *so* good," I purred, rolling my hips sexily. "I only wish you could be doing that to me a little bit lower."

"Except you've got no hair down there for me to wash," she smiled.

"Who needs hair," I said, hiking up my skirt to reveal my dripping pussy. "When you've got magical fingers like those?"

"I'd love to accommodate you," she said, glancing over at the line of customers occupying the full bank of styling chairs. "But I'm not sure we could get away with it in this open space. Although you might be able to slide your *own* hand under your skirt without being noticed while I give you a rub-down."

I quickly slipped my hand under my skirt, pressing two fingers into my hole as I peered up at Nikki.

"Fuck yes," I purred. "I'm going to get you to myself in this place one way or the other before long. I love getting off while you watch me, but I want to feel something other than a plastic vibrator rubbing up against me the next time you do my hair."

"Well then, today might be your lucky day," Nikki smiled, splashing the warm water softly over my forehead. "Because I've got something a little different in store for you while you get your hair styled."

"Oh?" I said, blinking my eyes as I spit the water playfully up toward her face. "Are you going to sit down with me on the chair and rub your pussy against mine?"

"Not this time," Nikki teased. "But I think what you'll experience will be as close to the real thing as you can get without someone actually being next to you."

"Fuck, Nikki," I panted while thrusting my fingers in and out of my sloshing pussy. "I don't know what I'm enjoying more, you massaging my head, or imagining what you've got waiting for me."

"You might want to save something for when you're in the *other* chair," she said, watching me rock my hips more rapidly approaching a climax. "I'd hate for you to waste a perfectly good orgasm when the *rest* of the girls could be enjoying it along with you."

"Okay," I said, pulling my fingers out of my dripping snatch while I licked my lips peering up at her. "But I'm only interested in *you* watching me come. I'm gonna fantasize it's you fucking me in the chair instead of a vibrator."

"Come on," Nikki said, spraying the warm water playfully over my face while she finished rinsing the conditioner out of my hair. "Let's go get you trimmed up while you experience a *different* kind of fingering."

As she led me over to the other salon chair, I felt my juices dripping all the way down to my calves in anticipation of what was in store. When we got to the chair, the other women sitting beside me smiled at me with lopsided grins knowing it was going to be something special.

"Anywhere in particular I should sit?" I said, glancing down at the slit in the seat.

"Sitting back is better than forward," Nikki smiled. "You can always adjust your position once the device engages."

"How does it *work* exactly?" I said, peering at the different controls on the armrest.

"The two-way arrow raises the vibrator up and down as far as you want. The up and down buttons work the same as before, adjusting the vibrator speed to the intensity you desire."

"It doesn't sound so different from the one I already used," I said with a puzzled look.

"Oh, this one is very different, I assure you," Nikki purred. "Feel free to activate it whenever you're ready."

I peered into the mirror, scanning the faces of the other women who were squirming in their chairs with soft flushes on their faces, then slowly pressed the top of the two-way arrow. Suddenly, a hard plastic dildo began rising out of the seat, pressing my folds apart as it entered my pussy.

"Huh!" I jumped up in my seat, not expecting the sudden intrusion.

"How's *that* for a realistic substitute?" Nikki smiled, peering at me in the mirror.

"You didn't tell me I'd be fucking a *male* surrogate this time," I panted, holding the button down as the phallus pressed deeper inside me.

"You're welcome to stop the device if it isn't working for you," Nikki kidded, parting my hair between her fingers while she started to snip it with her scissors.

"Are you *kidding* me?" I said, pressing my hips forward to engulf the hard phallus in my hole. "I'm so fucking horny right now, I could fuck a billygoat."

"Do you feel anything *besides* the dildo?" Nikki said, snipping the scissors calmly over my head.

My eyes suddenly flung open when I felt a pair of prongs sliding over my clitoris as the dildo pressed further inside me.

"Holy *fuck!*" I hissed, tilting my hips forward to push the prongs harder against my tingling nub.

"Remind you of any *other* toys you've used lately?"

"It feels vaguely similar to my rabbit vibrator with the vibrating ears for stimulating my clit," I nodded.

"Exactly," Nikki grinned. "Except this one also thrusts *up and down* while you're sitting still. Hold your finger over the middle of the arrow to see what I mean."

I moved my finger to the center of the arrow and suddenly the dildo began pushing up and down like some kind of automated fucking machine.

"Oh my God!" I gasped, gripping the armrests more tightly.

"Now you know what the pretty brunette was experiencing the last time you were in here," Nikki said.

"Unghh," I groaned, feeling my whole body being pushed up and down from the action of the pumping dildo. "This is *way* better than a Sybian machine. It's almost like I'm being fucked by a real man!"

"Or a woman," Nikki smiled. "Nowadays, it can be arranged it either way."

"What do the up and down buttons control?" I grunted, feeling my pussy juices beginning to spread over the leather seat.

"They adjust the speed of the vibrating prongs," Nikki said. "Give it a try. I think you'll find it takes the experience to a whole new level."

I pressed my finger over the Up button and suddenly the soft appendages on the base of the dildo began to flutter against the sides of my twitching clit.

"Mmfff," I groaned, pressing my pussy harder against the pumping dildo. "This is way better than a real cock. If only a man's penis was outfitted this way. They'd never have difficulty ever again making a woman come."

"I thought you'd like it," Nikki smiled, noticing the other women staring in the mirror watching me as they began to squirm more actively in their seats. "And from the look of it, so do the *rest* of my clients."

"Have most of them already given this one a turn?" I said.

"Yes," Nikki said, nodding while she met some of their gazes. "But I'm trying to spread the wealth around so everybody can give it a try."

"Why not outfit *all* of the chairs this way?"

"Like you said before, it's hard to cut a person's hair without making them look like Edward Scissorhands when they're hopping up and down in the chair this way. At least the *regular* vibrator keeps you relatively still in one place."

"I'll stop moving soon enough," I panted, feeling the familiar pangs of a powerful orgasm beginning to build up inside me. "I just need a few more seconds before I can tamp this thing back down."

"Knock yourself out, babe," Nikki smiled. "I'm happy to stop while you get your rocks off."

"Are you getting as excited as *I* am watching me getting fucked by this thing?"

"Not as much as I am imagining me fucking you *myself* the next time you're in here."

"Oh God, Nikki," I groaned. "You're going to make me come talking like that..."

"As if you need much help at this particular moment," she smiled, caressing my scalp with her fingers.

"Fuck, Nikki," I hissed. "I love feeling your hands on me. I'm going to come so hard..."

"Let it go, baby," Nikki said, digging her nails into my scalp. "Squirt your juices all over that big dildo while you imagine my fingers are rubbing your clit. Soon enough you'll feel my *whole* body pressed up against yours."

"Oh *fuck!*" I screamed out loud with my body tightening up as my pussy began clamping down on the thrusting dildo and I gushed all over the flapping prongs at the base of my clit.

As I shook in my seat with my apron fluttering from the action of my rocking hips, I watched in rising ecstasy while many of the other women lined up against the mirror came simultaneously, groaning along with me. For what seemed like an eternity, I rocked and rolled in my chair, held like a clamp by the hard piston pounding up and down inside me. I'd never felt such a powerful full-body experience being stimulated in so many places with so many people watching me come. When I finally stopped shaking, I paused the vibrator and slumped down in my seat, peering up at Nikki.

"I had no idea it was going to be this good when I suggested this idea to you a few weeks ago," I panted. "Who knew getting your hair done could be so much fun!"

5

After my experience on the thrusting dildo chair, I eagerly awaited my next appointment at the salon. As requested, Nikki scheduled me back-to-back behind the pretty brunette, who'd booked herself four weeks out. It took every ounce of my willpower not to visit the studio earlier hoping for a walk-on appointment or a cancelation. As cute as the brunette was, it was really *Nikki* who'd attracted my interest the most and whom I most wanted to fuck. When I entered the salon on my appointment day, I noticed that she was also wearing a short skirt instead of her customary jeans, and when she greeted me, she pressed her mound hard against mine when we kissed.

"Have you been trying out some of your own material?" I grinned, peering down at her sexy bare legs.

"As often as I can," she smiled, motioning to the full bank of chairs. "But there's limited opportunities with the place packed from opening to closing time. We're running a little behind schedule today, so unfortunately you'll have to wait for another twenty or thirty minutes." Then she clasped my hand, passing me a metal key. "Do you want to wait in the back room? We've got a coffee maker and a more comfortable lounge for you to rest on."

"Sure," I said. "As long as you'll join me soon."

"I've got a few clients I need to check up on, then I'll come by in a few minutes. Why don't you go ahead and relax? Just don't get any ideas while you're back there. I want you to save yourself for another earth-shaking orgasm on my special chair."

"I wouldn't *think* of it," I smiled, slapping her ass as I headed to the back room.

When I opened the door, I noticed a canvas-covered couch and a few other chairs, and a single stainless-steel sink with coffee machine. The coffee smelled fresh, so I went over to the counter and poured myself a cup, then sat down peering up at the photos of the pretty models on the wall. While I stared at their professional hair styles and gorgeous faces, I wondered if they were paid models or if they were real photos of the salon's clients.

Their blank expressions suggested they were professional models, and it didn't take long for my mind to wander back to the look on the pretty brunette's face while she sat in her chair with flushed cheeks and an expression of exquisite pleasure on her face. While I peered at the different photos of the models, I snaked my right hand under my skirt and began to play with my tingling clit. Soon after, Nikki swung open the door and when she saw me rubbing my pussy, she closed it quickly and sat down beside me, taking my coffee from my other hand and placing it on the floor.

"I thought you were going to save that for *me*?" she smiled, leaning in to kiss me.

"I was looking at your pretty models on the wall and thinking back to some of the faces of the women I saw the last time I was in here. You really should update these posters with some more current photos. You'd probably attract even *more* customers if they saw how happy your clients really are when they leave this place."

"Will *you* be my first model?" Nikki purred, slipping her hand under my skirt to caress my slippery folds. "I can't think of anyone as pretty or sexy. Besides, nobody looks hotter than you when you're in throes of pleasure."

"I dunno, babe," I grinned, lifting my leg and crawling on top of her lap. "I think *you* could give some of these models a run for their money too. I bet your clients would love to see the look of ecstasy on your face when you're coming as much as they enjoy watching the other customers."

"You've already seen me orgasm watching you," she said, grinding her hips against mine. "That's good enough for me."

"It's not good enough for *me*," I said, pushing her down onto the sofa and hiking up her skirt while peering at her pretty shaved pussy. "I've been dreaming about fucking you ever since you started massaging my wet head under your sink."

"That makes *two* of us," Nikki groaned as I positioned my pussy over hers in an upright scissor position.

"Oh Nikki," I moaned, feeling her wet lips pressing against mine. "I've been dying to feel your soft flesh against me..."

"Maybe I should make some new upgrades to the salon chairs," she smiled, reaching up to caress my breasts as I began to grind my pussy against hers.

"Unless *you're* sitting on the chair underneath me, I'm pretty sure you'll never be able to replicate the experience quite like this," I grunted.

"No, I suppose not," she panted, pulling off my blouse while she unclasped my bra behind my back. I did the same, throwing her blouse on the floor beside mine, and we pulled our bodies together, pressing our bare tits against one another while we thrust our tongues into each other's mouths.

"Fuck, baby," I groaned, pressing my tingling clit against her hard mound. "You're going to ruin me for your salon chairs after this. From now on, I'm only going to want to feel your wet cunt rubbing against me."

"We might be able to arrange that," Nikki said, suddenly pushing me backwards onto the sofa and bending my knees up to my chest as she straddled my hips and began humping her sopping pussy against mine.

"Yes, Nikki," I panted, peering up at her tits swinging above me while she rocked her hips against mine. "Fuck me like you *own* me.

You feel incredible."

"Even better than a vibrating plastic dildo?" she smiled, cocking an eyebrow.

"Like you said," I groaned, grabbing her tits while her clit rolled over mine. "A woman can do anything a man can do, only longer and better."

"Mmm," she said, leaning forward to press her torso against mine as she pushed my feet back even further behind my head. "And *wetter*. I want to feel you squirting all over my pussy instead of that plastic dildo. You're so fucking hot, I'm going to cum soon."

"Yes, baby," I grunted, feeling my own orgasm building up inside me like a runaway freight train. "Grind your pussy against me. I'm gonna gush all over your hot pussy."

"Oh *fuck*, Jade," Nikki wailed as she began to convulse overtop of me while breathing heavily into my mouth.

I grabbed the back of her ass with my hands and dug my nails into her cheeks while I tilted my hips forward, feeling my pussy beginning to clench open and shut. As it began pulsing in powerful contractions, I squirted my juices all over her gaping hole and exposed pucker. While my fountain washed over her ass and her lower back, we held onto each other tightly, shaking and groaning in each other's arms.

"How's *that* for a new kind of body wash?" I winked, peering into her eyes after we came down from our powerful climaxes.

"Way better than the regular massage at the sink," she smiled. "I might have to bring you back *here* next time for your styling prep from now on."

"That's *one* way to clean me up before I rest on your shaking seat," I said, feeling our combined juices rolling down over my slit and down my thighs.

Suddenly, the lunchroom door flipped open and three of Nikki's stylists peered in at the two of us still hunched over like two frogs caught humping each other.

"Can we get in on this action?" one of them said, closing the door softly behind them. "Everybody *else* in this place seems to be getting off except us. We heard you guys groaning back here and figured this might be a good time for a coffee break."

Nikki turned to look at me with a raised eyebrow, and I nodded, smiling.

"Why not?" she said, rolling off me and spreading her legs apart, inviting her colleagues to join the two of us. "It's not like the *rest* of the women won't have enough to keep themselves entertained while we amuse ourselves back here for a little while."

As the girls jumped onto the sofa and the five of us rolled around in a mangled twist of naked bodies sucking and humping each other's pussies, I couldn't help smiling at what I'd started. I had no idea when I suggested that Nikki consider upgrading her services that her salon would soon become known as the town's favorite place for lesbian orgies.

CIRCLE JERK

AN EROTIC ADVENTURE

VICTORIA RUSH

1

"Hi Han," I said, kissing my best friend and registered sex therapist, Hannah, on the cheek.

"Hey beautiful," she said, giving me a big hug. "How was your business trip?"

"Eventful," I said, taking a window seat at our favorite restaurant overlooking the Navy Pier.

We were meeting for our customary weekly downtown luncheon to get caught up, and I was eager to tell her about my latest adventure visiting Washington, DC.

"Never a dull moment with you, girl," she said, ordering a margarita when the waiter came to our table.

"You have no idea," I said, nodding to the waiter to double the order. "I almost got arrested this time."

"What?!" she said, almost spilling her water after taking a quick sip.

"Yeah, for *turning tricks*, no less."

"You *what*?" she said, coughing as her water went down the wrong way. "What the hell were you doing that for? It's not like you're suffering for sex these days. Or for money, for that matter."

"I kind of fell into it. A guy I picked up in a bar left me some money when we finished our business, thinking I was a hooker."

"Why did he think that?"

"Well, I was tarted up pretty good and maybe a little easier to get in the sack than usual..."

"How did that lead to your almost getting *arrested*?"

"After that first night, I started to wonder how much I could make if I really set my mind to it. So for the remainder of my stay, I decided to make a concerted effort to pick up new customers each night...."

"How much are we *talking* here?" Hannah said, pinching her eyebrows. "I thought the going rate was like fifty bucks for a blowjob and maybe a hundred for some quick intercourse."

"Not in one of the most expensive hotels in DC, it isn't. I ended up pulling in more than three G's for three nights' work."

"Holy shit!" Hannah said, taking a gulp of her margarita after the waiter returned with our drinks. "I'd almost give up my *counseling* job for that kind of money!"

"That's what I was thinking. It's highly addictive get paid to have sex. But I suppose I was pressing my luck going back to the same upscale bar every night. I think I was being watched by an under-cover cop."

"Did he have his way with you before he put the cuffs on you?"

"*She*. And yes she did. But there were no cuffs involved. I think she realized I was a new to this sort of thing and decided to give me a warning. But not before we fucked each other silly with a big pink dildo for the better part of two hours."

"You and your crazy escapades," Hannah said, shaking her head. "One of these days they're going to be your undoing."

"Maybe," I smiled. "But at least I'll die happy."

"How's everything going otherwise?"

"Pretty good. But I had a sex-related question I wanted to ask you today."

"About how not to get arrested while playing out your wildest fantasies?"

"No," I laughed. "It's about my increasing propensity to squirt and emit fluid when I have sex..."

"A lot of women would be *happy* to have your problem," Hannah chuckled, peering over the top of her glass as she licked the salty rim.

"That's kind of what I wanted to ask you about. Am I just a weirdo? Why do I seem to be the only one among my long list of female lovers who can do this?"

"Actually," Hannah said, placing her glass back down on the table. "*Every* woman has the ability to squirt when she comes. Most of the fluid comes from a special gland surrounding the urethra called the Skene's gland. It's somewhat equivalent to the male prostate gland insofar as it empties into the urethra if sufficiently stimulated and ejects through your pee hole. But most women have trained their pubococcygeus muscles to resist the flow because it feels like you're peeing when you release the fluid."

"So it's *not* actually pee?"

"No, it's a clear, mostly tasteless fluid. It actually helps with the reproductive function by providing useful nutrients for sperm to make their way up a woman's reproductive tract after a man ejaculates. If you go back far enough into the history of far Eastern cultures, there's a fairly robust record of women ejaculating when they had sex. It's only a recent phenomenon of our somewhat repressed Christian culture where women have been trained to withhold this natural phenomenon."

"Wow," I said, taking a healthy swig of my margarita. "I had no idea. How come I'm the only one who seems to have learned to unleash the beast, in a manner of speaking?"

"You have to be extraordinarily relaxed and at ease with your partner to feel comfortable coming all over them. Maybe it's because you mostly have sex with *women* now and there's no competitive pressure to see who can outsquirt who. Or maybe it's because you've had so many partners and you've learned how to release your waters."

"Hmm," I said, nodding as I began to feel my pulse return to normal. "So I'm not a deviant, then?"

"Far from it. You could almost argue that the women who *resist* their natural ability to ejaculate are the abnormal ones. I actually have a friend who conducts workshops teaching women how to do this."

"What, in *person*? Live and in the *buff*?"

"There's no other way. It gets pretty explicit actually. Part of the process is revealing exactly where your G-spot is and how to properly stimulate it."

"So, there's a bunch of women in these workshops spreading their pussies for one another to see while jilling themselves in full view of the other participants?"

"Exactly," Hannah said. "You might want to try it sometime. Besides being incredibly arousing, you might be able to teach some of the other girls a thing or two from your own successful experience."

"That's crazy," I said, suddenly intrigued about this masturbation seminar. "What's the name of your friend's workshop and how do I find her?"

"You can find her online. Search for Laila's Fountain of Venus Workshop."

"*Fountain of Venus*," I smiled. "What a lovely name for something I'd always found kind of dirty and embarrassing."

"Far from it. I think you'll find the experience quite liberating. It's all about reclaiming your natural female birthright and learning to express your sexuality fully."

When I got home, I flipped open my laptop and plugged in the search words, eager to learn more about this fascinating workshop. When the website came up, it was tastefully designed with beautiful pictures of Georgia O'Keefe erotic flowers and soft, romantic music. The homepage described how the workshop was transformative, helping women overcome negative body images and repressive attitudes to heal their bodies and learn to realize their full sexual potential.

As I clicked on the various links in the menu bar about 'Body Image', 'How to Orgasm', 'Understanding your G-Spot, and 'Freeing your Lotus Spring', I became more and more excited about attending one of the sessions. Although I didn't need help learning how to squirt myself, the idea of watching ten other women rubbing their pussies together and seeing them squirt in unison was incredibly exciting. The price wasn't cheap at one thousand dollars, but that included three full days including all meals and accommodation at a four-star hotel.

I clicked on the Schedule tab and frowned when I saw that the next four sessions were already booked. I'd have to wait more than a month to get in on the next available one in New York City. After entering my credit card information and contact details, I sat back in my chair, feeling my heart pumping excitedly in my chest. It would require another trip away from home, but this time *I'd* be the one paying to have sex, and it would be in a secure environment along with ten other consenting adults. I noticed a wet stain spreading in the crotch of my jeans and pulled off my clothes and spread my thighs, staring at my dripping vulva.

"Maybe you're not such a weirdo after all," I said, talking to my pussy as I placed two fingers inside my opening and began rubbing my swollen G-Spot. As I closed my eyes and imagined watching the other women rubbing their pussies while they watched me, I could already feel the familiar pangs of an oncoming ejaculation building up inside me.

2

———

On the day of my scheduled workshop, I packed excitedly and left early for my flight to La Guardia. The website had recommended I pack a comfortable robe, plenty of thick bath towels, lots of lube, a large makeup mirror, a flashlight, and my favorite sex toy. By the time I closed the suitcase, there was barely enough room for my regular clothes.

Shouldn't be a problem, I thought. *It's not like we're going to need any with a bunch of nude women sitting around a circle showing off their pussies all day.*

The workshop started at 1 p.m. the first day, so I checked into my hotel after I landed and threw some essentials into a tote bag then headed uptown to the address provided for the instructor's West Side co-op. When Laila greeted me at the door, I noticed a ring of reclining chairs arranged in a circle in the middle of her large living room overlooking Central Park. Her apartment was tastefully decorated with symbols of erotic art and sculpture, including a large Shunga painting of a naked Japanese woman appearing to pee into an urn while she massaged her vulva.

Some of the women had already arrived, and we awkwardly introduced ourselves while we sampled hors d'oeuvres laid out on a buffet table while soft instrumental music played in the background and a flowery incense permeated the room. Most of the participants had already changed into their robes, and as we chatted amongst ourselves, Laila circulated making small talk, trying to ease the nervous tension in the room. She was older than I expected, maybe in her early fifties, but beautiful with long gray hair, bright blue eyes, and a curvy Madonna-like figure that I couldn't help stealing glances at whenever her back was turned. When the last attendee arrived and we'd all changed into our robes, she asked us to take a seat in one of the lounges and make ourselves comfortable.

The lounge chairs were shaped in a flattened S-curve with a tight webbing of Gore-tex fabric to prevent staining and facilitate easy cleaning. The back and leg rests were sloped at the ideal angle to recline comfortably while still being able to view our own bodies and those of our seatmates easily. The whole atmosphere had an upscale hippie vibe to it, and I nodded at Laila's preparation, who obviously had conducted these workshops many times before.

"Thank you all for coming," she said, lying in the last empty lounge chair as some of the women chuckled at her unintended pun.

As I peered around the circle, I noticed the group included a wide range of ages, from a cute redhead looking to be somewhere in her early twenties to an attractive older woman in her late sixties. But most of them looked to be in their thirties and forties, with varying body shapes from slender and sylphlike to plump and rotund. While we all lay comfortably on our lounge chairs wearing nothing but body-hugging robes, I could feel the sexual tension in the room as the scent of feminine perfume mingled with the smoky incense.

"Feel free to help yourself to refreshments at any time," Laila said. "And if you haven't found them yet, there are two restrooms at the end of the corridor in the direction of the bedrooms. Is everybody feeling comfortable?"

"Mmm-hmm," the women murmured, nodding their heads enthusiastically.

"On this first afternoon of our three-day workshop, we're going to take things slow to start. Since this is all about overcoming the barriers to expressing our full feminine potential, I thought we'd begin with some introductions. If you feel comfortable, please share with us your purpose for attending, what you're hoping to gain from this workshop, and what impediments you've experienced in your journey of sexual exploration. And please don't be shy about sharing any of your feelings. This a safe environment where we're all here to support one another and learn from each other's experience. Am I right, ladies?"

"Absolutely," a pretty brunette in her thirties enthused.

"Okay then," Laila said. "Who'd like to start?"

A woman looking to be in her late forties raised her hand slowly and Laila nodded toward her.

"Yes, what is your name?"

"My name's Ava," the woman said. "I was hesitant about coming to this workshop, but a friend recommended it to me. My issue is that I've never been able to orgasm with a partner. My husband and I have been married for over twenty years, but during that time I've never come while having sex. I don't know if it's a mental block or if there's something wrong with me..."

"Thank you for sharing, Ava," Laila said. "First, I want you to know that there is nothing wrong with you and that this is a fairly common concern. The reasons for your inability to climax can have many sources. May I ask if you can orgasm through self-stimulation?"

"Yes..." the woman answered tentatively.

"That's a good sign," Laila nodded. "The reason for a woman's inability to orgasm with her partner is often grounded in expectations set by their family, or sometimes simply from the inexperience of your partner. Good open, honest communication between both partners is essential, but it starts with the understanding that it is normal, healthy, and perfectly natural for both partners to enjoy the sexual union together. We will address many of these issues in our workshop, and I'm confident you'll be able to elevate your sexual experience with your husband so that both of you enjoy your connection equally."

"Thank you," Ava said, unfolding her clamped arms over her chest and resting her hands in her lap.

"Who'd like to go next?" Laila said, peering around the circle.

The pretty brunette who'd interjected earlier raised her hand and Laila nodded toward her.

"My name's Claire," she said. "My reason for coming to the workshop is that I've been finding myself increasingly attracted to women, but I've been uncomfortable approaching them physically after so many years of failed heterosexual relationships. I thought by attending this seminar and seeing other women naked in a safe environment, it might help me break down the walls in a manner of speaking."

"Well, you've come to the right place, Claire," Laila said. "This is indeed a safe, nonjudgmental environment where all of us will be looking to become more comfortable in the presence of other women in a sexual context. I suspect others attending today share your motivation and that this forum will provide an uplifting introduction to the pleasures of same-sex discourse."

An African-American woman with a short afro raised her hand, and Laila nodded toward her.

"My name's Trinity, and I just wanted to tell Claire that as a proud lesbian since separating from my husband ten years ago, there's a whole new world of pleasure out there for you once you find a suitable partner. My purpose for attending the workshop is to learn new techniques for stimulating and arousing my partner. I find everybody's built differently and has different turn-ons, and I'm always looking for new ways to excite my lover."

"Indeed there is," Laila said. "And that's very well said, Trinity. Part of the purpose of this workshop from *my* perspective is to show that we all come in different shapes, sizes, and configurations, and that there is no one 'right' profile for becoming sexually actualized and learning to truly accept who we are."

Suddenly, a bunch of hands around the circle began to rise as the other women grew increasingly eager to share their goals and stories.

"Yes," Laila said, nodding toward a cute redhead in her mid-twenties.

"My name's Piper," she said. "My reason for coming to the workshop is that I've never been able to orgasm at *all*, from self-stimulation or partner sex. I don't know if you can help me, but I just want to learn what it actually feels like to come any way I can."

"Thank you for sharing, Piper," Laila nodded. "This is a more common phenomenon than many women realize. I want to assure you that you're not alone, and that learning to orgasm can be a transformative experience. We will be taking our time at first to explore our bodies in order to become fully comfortable and relaxed. Every woman has the ability to orgasm, and once you learn how, there's never any going back!"

The rest of the women in the room chuckled as more hands flew up in the air.

"Yes," Laila said, nodding toward a pretty Hispanic woman in her early forties.

"My name's Carla, and I'm not going to lie. My main reason for coming to this workshop is to learn how to squirt! No matter how much I try or how many online videos I watch, I can never seem to make it happen. Your website mentioned this was something we were going to explore, and I'm eager to see if you can help me."

"Yes, Carla," Laila chuckled. "That's one of the things we will explore towards the second half of our workshop. You may actually be surprised to know that *every* woman is equipped with the tools and anatomy to ejaculate. Much like other forms of sexual expression, it begins with accepting this is a normal and healthy part of your sexual experience and learning the proper technique to turn on your Lotus Spring.

"Who'd like to go next?"

A hot-looking blonde in her forties suddenly interjected.

"While we're on the subject of female ejaculation, I'd like to share my goal of learning how to make my *lover* squirt. My name's Hailey, and I've never really had a problem with ejaculating myself, but no matter how hard I try, I just can't seem to produce the same fireworks with my girlfriend. She's actually become somewhat self-conscious about it and I was hoping to bring back some new techniques to help her turn the corner."

By the time all the women had finished introducing themselves, everybody had become more relaxed, laughing and supporting one another while we shared our goals and sexual frustrations. When my turn came, I explained that I'd simply come with an open mind to learn some new techniques, not wanting to share that really I was just excited to watch a bunch of other hot women masturbating openly. Laila introduced herself last, explaining that she'd been a sex therapist and counsellor for many years, but that she'd found these live workshops were the best way to help women overcome their sexual blocks and become fully actualized.

After a short refreshment break, she lit some candles to set the mood for the next stage in our journey of erotic self-exploration.

"Now that we've gotten to know one another a little better and shared our goals, the next step is to bare *another* piece of ourselves by disrobing. The purpose of this step is to learn more about our own bodies and to appreciate that every woman is built differently. The first step in realizing our full potential is recognizing the inner and outer beauty that we all share regardless of our skin color, body type, or sexual persuasion. To that end, whenever you feel comfortable, I'd like you to remove your robe and lay down on your chaise chair completely naked. You may wish to place some towels underneath you, as inevitably there will be some bodily fluids involved."

As everyone slowly removed their robes and placed them in their bags beside them on the floor, it became more apparent that each of the women had a different body shape and size. Some of the women were rotund with rolls around their bellies and large pendulous breasts, some were slender with barely perceptible tits, and others were curvy and voluptuous with sexy hips and proud bouncing boobs. Some of them lay confidently on their reclining chairs with their bodies fully exposed and their legs slightly parted revealing the dark slit in their pussies, while others lay more demurely with their legs pressed tightly together and their arms crossed over their chest trying to protect their modesty. I peered over at Laila, who'd joined the rest of the group lying buck naked, and I felt my pussy moistening while I soaked up her curvy, well-toned body.

"Right then," she smiled with a twinkle in her eye. "That wasn't so difficult, was it?"

Everybody laughed nervously while squirming in their chairs.

"The first thing I want you to do is peer around the circle and notice how each of us is built differently. There is no one standard size or shape for a woman, and we should revel in the uniqueness that defines each of us while at the same time admiring the wonderful disparity in the female form. Isn't it marvelous to see the exciting differences between us and realize that, like a snowflake or an individual flower, there are no two that are alike?"

Each of us peered around the circled and nodded in appreciation at the smorgasbord of feminine beauty laid out before us.

"Like good food, it's the *variety* that makes our experience as women truly interesting and satisfying. Can you imagine always eating chocolate cake for dessert or having waffles with maple syrup for breakfast every day? As lovely and appetizing as these dishes may be, we would soon tire of them and they'd lose their allure if that was all we ever had to experience. I want you to take a moment to bask in the innate beauty of each of your colleagues and soak up their unique body styles so that we can fully appreciate the inherent beauty within each of us. Let's give a round of applause to recognize the unique beauty that all of us share."

While Laila began to clap softly, the group slowly joined in, until thunderous applause filled the room as we all peered around the circle beaming at one another with broad smiles.

"Yes, indeed," Laila said, nodding approvingly. "We are all beautiful and unique in our own special way. But one thing we all have in *common* is that we are all proud owners of that wonderful part of our anatomy called our vulvas. The fount of life itself, this amazing organ is capable of giving us incredible pleasure, unifying us with our partners, and bringing new life into this world. And just as with the *other* parts of our bodies, each woman's vulva is shaped and configured differently.

"If you feel comfortable, I'd like you to begin spreading your legs apart to reveal your sacred temple and notice how each of our vulvas have a different shape, color, and configuration. Just as with the rest of our body, there is no one perfect pussy. Like a blossoming flower, our folds and contours are shaped differently, and it is our multiplicity that makes each of us special and interesting. Raise your knees up and take a long moment to peer at your beautiful pussy, touching and stretching your folds to examine it carefully. Celebrate your womanhood and accept that you are the best possible *you* you can be. Proudly show your colleagues around the circle your exquisite yoni and don't be ashamed of your unique configuration. Every one of us is different, and every one of us is beautiful!"

As we all peered around the room staring at each other's pussies, I was fascinated by the incredible diversity of colors, shapes, and sizes. I'd been with a lot of women in my life, but somehow seeing the ten of us fully exposed with our cunnies framed by our spread legs on the low-lying lounges truly revealed the wide range of morphology that we all shared. Some of the women's pussies had dark brown labia while others had pink or pale white lips. Some of the lips were full and puffy, and some were thin and tight. Some hung in convoluted folds like a piece of drapery resting on the floor, whereas others were strung as tight as a freshly tuned lute.

Some women had hairy bushes, some had neatly trimmed pubic mounds, and some, like me, were totally bald. In some of the women's vulvas I could clearly see their clitoris standing tall and proud, a pink bulb poking out from its protective hood like a little piggy in a blanket, whereas in other women it was neatly concealed under the fold of skin at the top of their slits. It was strangely *non-erotic* taking it all in, and I was utterly mesmerized by the spectacle of it all.

"This is one of my favorite moments," Laila said, smiling broadly as she watched each of the women appraising each other's vulvas and nodding approvingly. "When we can revel in the common beauty that defines us as women and embrace the differences that make each of us unique. Now, I want you to take a closer look at your beautiful yonis by taking out the mirrors I asked each of you to bring with you, as well as your flashlights. If it's a lighted makeup mirror that you brought, plug it into the extension cord resting beside each of your lounges. If not, point your flashlight so that it shines directly on your vulva and position your mirror so you can see your flower from the perspective of an imaginary lover."

It took each of us a few minutes to get everything set up properly and to position our bodies and mirrors to see our pussies close up, but when we did, I heard some audible gasps and deep breathing coming from my seatmates. For many of the women, it was obvious this was the first time they'd looked at their pussies this close-up.

"Take a moment this time to truly examine every part of your magnificent vulva," Laila said. "Spread your lips apart and examine the space between your labia. Notice the size and shape of your clitoral bulb and hood, find the position of your urethral opening between your clit and your vagina, and pinch your thick outer labia and thinner inner labia. Slide your fingers all the way down your pudendum and along the edges of your labia as you bask in the sights and sensations of this most amazing part of a woman's anatomy. Squeeze your pelvic muscles and notice how your skin flexes all the way from the top of your vulva to your anus. Watch how your pussy moistens as you touch it and spread it apart, like a beautiful flower blossoming with dew in the springtime. You are truly one of a kind and incredibly beautiful in every way."

I'd spent enough time peering at my own and other woman's pussies over the past few years, but I'd never really taken the time to clinically analyze the shape and configuration of my cunny, nor those of other women for that matter. As I stared at my tiny pee hole while I stretched and squeezed my lips, watching it flex open and shut, I shook my head marveling at all the parts I'd never paid attention to, amazed at the complexity and unifying beauty of my female instrument.

After a few minutes, I looked up and noticed all the other women staring at their pussies with equal wonderment and awe, every one of them with huge smiles on their faces while they reveled in their unique beauty. Even though none of us had so much as *tried* to stimulate ourselves sexually, it was one of the most exciting and uplifting experiences I'd ever experienced in the company of other women.

When Laila ended the session about thirty minutes later, inviting all of us to her favorite restaurant later that evening, I noticed a certain glow and contented smile in the women as we said our temporary goodbyes upon leaving her apartment. I had no idea what was in store for the rest of our three-day workshop, but I'd already gained a new appreciation for my sexual instrument as well as that of my female partners, and I found myself walking with a happy lilt as I flagged a cab to head back to my hotel.

3

———————

W e all enjoyed a delicious sushi dinner later that evening, laughing and learning much more about each of our histories, predilections, and erotic desires. By the time we all headed back to our hotels around 10 p.m., everybody was far more relaxed and comfortable about sharing our sexual experiences. That night, I had a strange dream where I was shrunken to the size of a dildo while I buzzed in front of Laila's vulva as she masturbated herself to orgasm. I had no idea what the meaning of the dream was, but I certainly woke up eager to see more of our attractive workshop leader's pussy close-up.

The following morning, we all showed up at her apartment at 9 a.m. and quickly disrobed, assuming our usual positions on the reclining lounges. I noticed this time that all of the women were more comfortable about revealing their pussies, spreading their legs wide apart as they proudly showed off their erotic flowers.

"I hope everybody had a restful night," Laila said, lying naked on her lounge two positions to my left. "Today we're going to explore our beautiful vulvas more closely and learn more about what goes on *inside* our vaginas, especially with regard to the mysterious G-Spot. As we will see, the G-Spot holds many wonderful surprises, including the magical wellspring of waters that allows us to express our full feminine potential.

"But first, we're going to baseline our erotic experience by masturbating in our familiar manner. This is where you're welcome to use the vibrators that you brought with you, or if you prefer, simply use your hand to stimulate yourself. As with yesterday, I don't want anybody to feel self-conscious in any way. We're all here to support one another and enjoy the shared experience. So without any further ado, feel free to spread your legs and enjoy yourselves."

We all looked at one another for a moment, then each of us reached into our tote bags, removing our favorite vibrators. I recognized many familiar toys that I'd used myself, including the popular Rabbit, Magic Wand, and Pocket Rocket. But when I pulled out my Osé vibrator, the women peered at me with a curious look on their faces, having never seen the strange-looking device. Formed in the shape of a hand, the 'palm' had a large opening where a tongue-like appendage flapped against my clit, and a long, curved finger which flexed inside me to stimulate my G-Spot.

While everybody checked their batteries and plugged in their devices, I noticed Laila slipping the C-shaped We-Vibe device into her slit, pulling it tightly against her vulva as the other women began caressing their pussies. As the whirring and humming noises began to fill the room, I could hear soft moans emanating around the circle as the women began to spread their legs further apart and rolled their hips in escalating pleasure.

I slipped the finger of the Osé vibrator inside me and tapped the remote-control device to activate the undulating tongue action and groaned at the familiar feeling of the slippery appendage lapping against my flaring clit. I'd used the device many times before, but watching ten other women playing with their pussies at the same time raised my pleasure tenfold. I was mesmerized peering around the circle, seeing how each woman used their devices and watching the rising look of ecstasy on their faces.

Ava, the woman who couldn't come with her husband, held her magic wand tightly between her legs with two hands, tilting her hips upwards as she pressed the industrial-strength vibrator hard against her clit.

No wonder she couldn't climax with her husband, I thought. If that's the way she's become accustomed to orgasming, who could possibly compete with that?

Claire, the woman around my age who'd confessed to being newly attracted to women, used a plain pink vibrating dildo, sliding it slowly between her lips while she stared wide-eyed at the other women rubbing their pussies beside her. Carla, the attractive Hispanic woman who said she wanted to learn how to squirt, used the small but powerful Pocket Rocket vibrator to focus all of the unit's power directly on her clit as her mouth gaped open in pleasure.

Trinity, the pretty African-American lesbian who said she wanted to learn new techniques for stimulating her partner, inserted her big Rabbit vibrator deep into her hole while she pulled her legs together and rammed the dildo in and out of her cunt. Piper, the cute redhead who said she'd never been able to orgasm at all, used her right hand to massage her vulva while she stared at the strange collection of electronic devices the other women were using to stimulate themselves.

I peered over at Laila and noticed that she was resting fairly still on her lounge chair as she quietly pressed the base of her vibrator harder against her pussy. She seemed to be watching the other women intently, like she was *studying* their technique rather than losing herself in her own pleasure as her vibrator hummed silently inside her.

But as the moans and groans of the other women began to grow more prominent, I felt my own pleasure beginning to rise, and I switched on the flexing finger action of the Osé vibrator, feeling it rubbing against the base of my G-Spot. It was obvious that many of the women were nearing their climaxes as their bodies began to tense and their grip on their vibrators grew tighter.

Trinity was the first to pop off as she grabbed the base of her

Rabbit vibrator and pulled it hard against her vulva with two hands, shaking vigorously as her whole body jerked and spasmed on the reclining chair. Soon after, Ava came, as a deep rash spread over her chest and her mouth gaped open in the throes of climax while she held her big vibrator hard against her dripping pussy.

Overcome by the sight of the other women coming, Claire couldn't hold back any longer as she thrust her skinny dildo deep into her snatch and flapped her thighs in and out, moaning loudly along with the others. Carla was the next one to lose control, as she lifted her hips high off the base of her chair, pressing the chrome nubs of her Pocket Rocket hard against her clit while her pelvic floor muscles pulsed in a series of powerful contractions.

By now, Piper was rubbing her vulva furiously with her hand, trying desperately to get off with the other women, but as her whole body flushed near the tipping point, she suddenly stopped, breathing heavily in her chair with a disappointed look on her face.

The last one to come before I did was Hailey, the hot blonde in her forties who'd said she didn't have any trouble squirting, but that she'd come to the workshop to learn how to make her partner ejaculate. Her technique was a little different from most of the other girls, employing both of her hands to stimulate her pussy instead of a vibrator. As her right hand circled her engorged clitoris, she curled two fingers of her other hand inside her pussy, rubbing the entrance of her hole rapidly while she clenched her buttocks and slowly lifted her ass off the surface of her chair. As her moans grew progressively louder, she let out a loud yelp and pulled her fingers out of her cunt, squirting high up into the air in a series of powerful gushes.

I peered over at Laila who was nodding as she watched Hailey coming, then she turned toward me just as I began to feel my own body tightening on the brink of climax. As I spread my legs wide apart and began to jet my fluids out the side of my pussy onto my quivering thighs, she pressed her curved vibrator harder against her pussy, jerking softly in her chair while we shared a long, simultaneous orgasm.

When all of the grunting and moaning finally stopped, the

women peered around the circle and began to laugh. This was probably the first time any of us had done something this audacious, and after seeing how much fun it was witnessing other women releasing their sexual inhibitions together, all we could do was laugh at how wonderfully liberating it felt.

4

———

After we all cleaned up and replaced the wet towels underneath us, Laila pulled the We-Vibe vibrator out of her pussy and placed it on the floor beside her chair.

"Well that certainly looked like fun," she smiled. "What do you think, girls, did you enjoy that?"

"Oh yeah," Hailey said, still patting down the insides of her wet thighs and ass.

"Definitely," Trinity said.

"Oh my God," Claire enthused. "That was the hottest thing I've ever experienced!"

"Did you find this to be a relaxed introduction to having sex with other women?" Laila smiled.

"I'm not sure *relaxed* is the right word," she said, still trying to collect her breath. "It looks like I've got a long way to go to catch up with everybody when it comes to using the latest toys."

"Vibrators can be a fun addition to your sex life," Laila nodded. "There's certainly an abundance of different shapes and designs to satisfy anyone's curiosity. But sometimes the greatest pleasure can be had by using our fingers and other parts of our bodies to stimulate ourselves and our lovers."

Laila peered over in Piper's direction and smiled.

"How about you, Piper? How did you find the experience?"

"It was incredibly arousing watching all the other women stimu-lating themselves and coming so powerfully. I could feel my body tingling all over, but I still don't think I came."

"You'd certainly know if you did," Laila said. "But don't worry. Learning to orgasm takes longer for some women than others. As we saw yesterday, everybody is different, and every woman has a different sexual history. The key is learning how to relax and enjoying the *journey* rather than focusing entirely on the destination. When you're ready, it will definitely come."

"I hope so," she said. "Because judging by the expressions of the other women around the room, I'm definitely ready for some of that."

As the rest of the group chuckled, Laila reached down beside her, placing an unusual object on her lap.

"I noticed while I was watching each of you that most of you concentrated on stimulating the *external* part of your vulva. But did you know that the clitoris is actually much larger and goes much deeper than you might believe?"

She held the plastic object up in the air and turned it slowly for each of us to see. Looking a bit like an oversize praying mantis, it had a long pointed 'nose' and large flappy wings extending out from its body.

"This is a scale model of an actual clitoris, showing both the *external* parts we're all familiar with, and the *internal* parts that comprise the bulk of the structure."

She slid her finger along the protruding proboscis, caressing her way down over the flaring wings of the model.

"Like the tip of an iceberg, the clitoral glans and shaft that we see on the outside of our vulva only represents a tiny fraction of this magnificent organ. The rest of your clitoris rests *inside* your vagina, spreading out and surrounding the walls of your tunnel with sensi-tive, erectile tissue that provides its own kind of unique pleasure when properly stimulated. So, in a way, there's no such thing as a clitoral vs. vaginal orgasm–they're actually the same thing. Whether you orgasm from internal or external stimulation or a combination of the two, different parts of your clitoris are being stimulated either way."

"Why can't I come with my husband when we have intercourse then?" Ava said, crossing her arms in frustration.

"The glans of our clitoris, which is what we're most familiar with on the outside of our vulva, has the most concentrated nerve endings and it can be easy for some of us to focus our attention there, since it's often the easiest and surest way to get off. But if we become too acclimated to reaching orgasm purely from external stimulation, sometimes it can be difficult to train ourselves to enjoy the process of penetration with our partners. But there's *another* organ inside our vaginas that has the power to take our pleasure to a whole new level. And that is our *G-Spot*. How many of you have heard of the G-Spot?"

Virtually every woman around the circle raised their hands without hesitation.

"How many of you know where it is?"

Most of the women raised their hands, but more tentatively this time.

"Would anybody like to explain?"

Trinity raised her hand and Laila nodded for her to speak.

"It's on the inside of our vaginas on the upper wall, close to our pubic bone."

"That's true," Laila said. "Do you exactly how *far* inside?"

"I'm not a hundred percent sure," Trinity said. "Towards the back?"

"Actually, the G-Spot, like the clitoris, is quite a bit larger and shaped differently than many of us have been led to believe. It's an egg-shaped bump that starts about two inches inside our vagina and tapers toward the back of the cavity. We can actually see it with the right equipment and technique. How many of you would like to see your G-Spots for the first time?"

"Yes, please!" Carla interjected excitedly.

"Okay," Laila said. "Take out your flashlights and mirrors once again and position them in front of your vulvas like we did yesterday."

Laila waited a few minutes until everybody was properly set up, then she moved her own mirror to the side so everyone could see her pussy clearly from around the circle.

"Follow along with me as I show you the simple steps for revealing this amazing organ."

Laila placed the index finger of each hand gently inside her hole then slowly pulled her lips apart.

"Place a finger from each hand inside your vagina and slowly spread it apart until you can clearly see your vaginal opening. Now, push your pelvic floor muscles forward like you're bearing down to deliver a baby. You'll see the tissue inside your vagina begin to press out. Continue until you see a little bump on the top of your vagina with horizontal ridges running across its surface..."

As Laila demonstrated the technique, our eyes all bulged out when we saw the protruding bump clearly highlighted by her flashlight.

"That little swelling with the horizontal ridges is your G-Spot," she said. "Isn't it magnificent? Now you try it."

The room became so silent you could hear a pin drop as the rest of the women followed Laila's instructions, peering intently into their propped-up mirrors while they stretched their labia apart. Suddenly, one woman after another gasped when she saw her G-Spot up close and personal for the first time. As I gaped at my own in wonderment, I could hardly believe that I'd never actually *seen* it after so much experimenting with sex with other men and women.

"It's pretty incredible, isn't it?" Laila said, smiling broadly as she panned around the room peering at all the women staring at their pussies with wide eyes.

"Now insert the two middle fingers of your primary hand into your opening and feel the shape and size of your G-Spot."

She demonstrated the technique for everyone else to see as she sunk the two middle fingers of her right hand into her pussy, pressing her two outer fingers up against the side of her thighs.

"Run your two fingers along the trough on the side of the bulge, squeezing it gently between your fingers. Can you feel how it's spongy, almost like a water-filled balloon?"

Many of the women nodded as they turned their hands slowly with their fingers embedded inside their pussies.

"Feel the ridges on the leading edge of your G-Spot, where it's most prominent. Notice that it's only one-and-a-half to two inches inside your vagina. Now, still squeezing it gently between your two fingers, press your fingers deeper inside your pussy, noticing how the bulge tapers off toward some soft, fluffy tissue about four inches inside."

Laila reached down beside her then passed a picture around the circle showing an object that looked like the cotton-candy sticks at the fair.

"Unknown to many women," she continued. "This bulge inside the front of your vaginas is actually a separate *organ* called the Skene's gland. The Skene's gland is somewhat equivalent to a man's prostate, even sharing a similar chemical makeup containing an enzyme called prostate specific antigen, or PSA. The fluid inside this gland, which is what causes the bulge inside your vagina, produces a clear, colorless liquid that empties into your urethra and is emitted through your pee hole."

"Is this where a woman's *ejaculate* comes from?" Piper said, shaking her head in amazement.

"Primarily, yes," Laila nodded. "But because it feels like you're about to pee when it's expressed, most women have trained themselves to hold it in when they orgasm by contracting their pelvic floor muscles."

"So it's not actually *urine* even though it comes out the same hole?" Claire said.

"No," Laila said. "I'm going to teach your how to express this gland in a few minutes and you'll see that it has a completely different color, smell, and chemical composition than urine. In fact, scientists have recently discovered that the fluid emitted by this gland facilitates contraception by providing essential nutrients for sperm as they make their way up the reproductive tract after ejaculation."

"So, if a woman ejaculates at the same time as her husband, it actually *increases* the chances of conception?" Carla asked. "Why haven't we been taught about this in our sex education classes? The discussion always seems to focus on the *man's* role in inseminating the woman with his sperm!"

"I'm not entirely sure," Laila said, nodding her head sympathetically. "Maybe it's because until fairly recently women weren't encouraged to enjoy sex, let alone to the extent they could ejaculate in a manner similar to men. It may also be a product of our repressed Western culture. For thousands of years, other cultures have known about, encouraged, and even celebrated the natural ability of every woman to ejaculate. Many of them would spread the waters upon their bodies or even *drink* it, believing it had magical healing qualities."

"Is that what the woman in the illustration on the wall is doing?" Trinity asked, peering at the Japanese Shunga painting.

"Exactly. This painting created many centuries ago depicts a woman ejaculating into an urn while she's stimulating herself. Far from being embarrassed about the release of her female fluid while she's having sex, she doesn't want to waste a precious drop."

"Can you teach us how to do this too?" Trinity said.

"Absolutely," Laila said. "Now that you know exactly where your G-Spot is and how to manipulate it, it's actually quite easy. You can even do it without climaxing. Let's take it in baby steps. First let's learn how to express it, then we'll learn how to squirt when we orgasm, which you'll find takes your erotic experience to a whole new level of satisfaction."

Holy shit, I thought to myself. *Hannah wasn't kidding when she said this workshop would be enlightening.* I had no idea there was so much history and science behind the act of squirting, and I couldn't wait to try it out with my newfound friends.

5

———————

Laila ordered sandwiches in for lunch, but it must have been the shortest meal any of us had had in a long time, we were all so excited to learn how to use our newfound G-Spots. When we resumed our positions on our lounge chairs, all the women still had their mirrors propped up expectantly between their legs. But Laila told us to put them away, since the next exercise would be guided mostly by feel. As I peered around the circle at everyone's naked body, I was happy to have an unobstructed view to watch the impending waterworks.

"Right, then," Laila said, taking her seat. "Your first order of business is to place extra towels underneath you, perhaps even doubling them under your butt. You'll be surprised how much fluid this gland can eject, up to five times as much as a man ejaculates when he comes."

Far from being irritated at Laila's frequent comparisons to men, I appreciated how it made us feel empowered about our own sexuality and that we should no longer feel like we were taking a back seat to their enjoyment.

"But I also don't want you to feel any reluctance to let your femi-nine waters flow," Laila said. "Both the hardwood floors and the vinyl-covered chairs can be easily cleaned. The first step in learning to ejaculate is removing any mental barriers to letting it all hang out, figuratively speaking."

Everyone giggled while we nodded excitedly.

"The one thing you'll need to get started is a little bit of lube. Although you'll be producing plenty of moisture by the time we finish, you'll want to make it easy to insert your fingers and massage your G-Spots with a minimum of friction. So place a healthy dollop on your two middle fingers while you lift your knees to a ninety-degree angle."

While everyone assumed the position, the women suddenly fell silent, as an electric charge filled the room.

"Before we actually begin massaging our G-Spots, first I want to conduct a little test. We're going to check the strength and elasticity of your perineal muscles."

Laila cupped her hands together with a small space between her palms.

"These are a pair of hammock-shaped muscles that run all the way from your pubic bone at the top of your vulva to your coccyx near your anus. Their primary role is to support your pelvic organs, but they also play a critical role in a woman's sexual and reproductive health. If they're too *tight*, this can cause pain in your pelvic region, and if they are too *loose*, this can contribute to incontinence."

"Is that why I frequently have pain in my lower abdomen when I have sex with my husband?" Claire asked.

"Possibly," Laila nodded. "Particularly if his penis is larger than most men's, or he's rough when you have sex. This can cause painful bruising of the cervix, which many women instinctively try to resist by clamping down on their PC muscles in an effort to control their partner's penetration. Over time, this chronic contraction of the perineal muscles causes cramping and other types of referred pain."

"He *is* quite large," Claire said. "But how else can I counteract his tendency to thrust so deeply inside me?"

"As with all healthy sex between partners," Laila said. "It starts with good, open, honest communication. When you explain the consequences of his actions, any loving husband should be willing to adjust his technique to please his partner. There are plenty of other ways for him to enjoy the act of sex, but it starts with him resisting the temptation to penetrate you fully, at least until he ejaculates. Besides, I have a feeling when you show him your new powers to squirt during sex, this will more than make up for any other concessions he might have to make. Most men, and women for that matter, get quite turned on seeing their partner ejaculate."

Many of the women chuckled, reflecting on the many porn videos they and their husbands had undoubtedly watched with the women squirting all over their partners when they came.

"Okay, now press your two fingers into your vaginal opening up to the first joint," Laila said. "Then squeeze them gently with your PC muscles. You should be able to insert them fairly easily, with a snug, but not overly tight fit. If you have difficulty squeezing them, your PC muscles may be too weak, whereas if you have difficulty pressing them inside or they feel too tightly compressed, your PC muscles may be too tense."

"What do we do if they're too weak?" Molly, the sixty-year-old woman said.

"Like any muscle, they atrophy from lack of use and can be strengthened with proper exercises. Simply contracting them often and attempting to hold your finger or other objects in your vagina will help. There are also a variety of PC muscle aids like Ben-Wa balls and vaginal barbells that you can buy to facilitate the strengthening process. It's especially important the older we get to keep these muscles well maintained, to avoid urinary problems."

"Can you show me where to buy these aids?" Molly asked.

"I'll leave each of you with a summary of links to reference and purchase most of the items I discuss during this workshop. But for now, simply understand that this is something that can be fairly easily fixed and improved."

"I seem to have the *opposite* problem," Claire said, frowning as she flexed her arm muscles while pressing her fingers inside her vagina.

"I can barely get my fingers inside. It almost feels like I have a tourni-quet around them."

"This is usually more of a *mental* problem than a physical one," Laila nodded. "The first step is learning to relax your PC muscles, realizing that you are in a safe zone where nobody can hurt you. Close your eyes and breathe slowly and deeply, concentrating on relaxing all the muscles in your pelvic region. Can you feel the pressure beginning to ease up on your fingers?"

"Yes," Claire said.

"Okay, now that we know how to optimize our PC muscles' strength and flexibility, let's begin to *stimulate* our G-Spot to make it engorged and full of fluid. Insert your two fingers a little deeper, up to the second joint until you feel the horizontal ridges of your gland, then press gently on the bump, massaging it gently in small circles."

Everybody closed their eyes while their hands moved slowly inside their pussies.

"Relax while you concentrate on the pleasurable sensations you're feeling. After a few minutes, you may feel the familiar sensation of an approaching orgasm, and the roof of your vagina will begin to balloon near the far end. If so, I want you to slow down and concentrate on your breathing. This first time we're going to learn to ejaculate *without* orgasm, then we'll make it a little more exciting by adding an erotic element to it."

As Laila instructed each of us what to do, she closed her eyes while she moved her fingers inside her pussy. I watched her pretty face and her rising and falling breasts, feeling my G-Spot becoming increasingly swollen and more aroused.

"Can you feel your G-Spot becoming engorged?"

"Yes," Ava said as the other women nodded silently.

"As you continue to stimulate your G-Spot, you'll begin to feel the sensation of needing to urinate. This is a good thing. Don't worry, you will not actually *pee*. There is an entirely different set of muscles that control the release of urine. As the urge to pee continues to build up inside you, begin to push out with your PC muscles like you did yesterday when you first examined your G-Spot. Hold it for a few seconds, then stop pushing but continue stimulating your G-spot. This will help to build up your ejaculatory juices. Your G-Spot should feel quite hard and swollen now."

"Yes," Carla panted. "I can feel it. Should I let it go now?"

"When you feel like you can't hold it any longer, remove your fingers from your opening and bear down. Don't clamp your PC muscles to *tighten* them, push to *release* like you're delivery a baby. As you begin to feel fluid coming out of your urethra, keep pushing. Remember, you are not peeing, you are *ejaculating* from your female prostrate. Release the spring and revel in your new feminine powers. Feel comfortable jetting your fluid all over your legs and your pussy while you ejaculate."

I turned in the direction of Laila and saw that her buttocks were clamped tightly together while jets of clear fluid began pulsing out of her vulva in long and powerful streams.

"Oh!" Carla suddenly huffed, as her pussy began gushing a waterfall over her bare vulva and ass.

"Huh!" Claire exclaimed as she arched her back and jets began squirting from her elevated pussy.

"Oh my God!" Piper exclaimed as her pretty cunny began to express the clear fluid from her prostate.

One after another, every woman around the circle began to jet their ejaculate from their pussies, sighing and grunting in delight at their newfound ability to come on demand. Up to this point, I'd been holding mine in but when I saw all the others spraying all over their bodies and lounge chairs, I pulled my fingers out of my hole and proudly squirted my juices halfway across the room. For the first time in my life, I'd ejaculated without orgasm and it felt incredibly empowering, like I'd just discovered some kind of new superpower.

Talk about the Fountain of Venus, I smiled, watching the women tilting their hips so they could better watch the jets of liquid arcing out of their pussies. *That's the sexiest fountain I've ever seen.*

6

After all of the women had finished ejaculating, we all lay still on our lounges, not even bothering to clean up the mess we'd made spraying all over our bodies and the surrounding furniture. It was as if everybody wanted to revel in the feeling of their juices bathing their bodies, much like the afterglow after orgasm.

"Holy shit!" Ava said. "That was incredible. I've never been able to do that, and I didn't even climax!"

"Same here," Carlo said. "Finally–I can come like a *man!*"

Everybody laughed while we clapped our hands together, thrilled for ourselves and all the others that we'd been able to express this new dimension of our sexual powers.

"Yes," Laila nodded. "Isn't it liberating to know that we can express our full feminine powers whenever we want and no longer feel guilty about enjoying the sexual response to the fullest? For those of you in a *heterosexual* relationship, I think your partners will be surprised and delighted with your newfound ability to ejaculate. And for those of you in lesbian relationships, your partners will be *equally* excited and turned on with your shower of love."

"It felt wonderful," Piper nodded. "But I feel like I still haven't experienced a proper orgasm. When will we be able to experiment with this new technique and learn to *climax* at the same time?"

"I'm glad you asked, Piper," Laila said, passing around a box of tissues. "Because that will be the next step in our journey of self-exploration. First, why don't we all take a little break to collect our breath and clean up? But before we do, I'd like each of you to take a tissue and blot up some of the ejaculate you just emitted. Then if you really have to go pee, while you're in the restroom compare the smell and appearance of the two fluids. We'll discuss the results when we reconvene. If you thought that *last* exercise was liberating, wait until we add the sexual element to the equation. See you all again in fifteen minutes."

While we all cleaned up our seating arrangements and placed new towels down on our lounges, Laila put on some sexy music and replaced the incense burning in the room with a new, musky scent. When we all returned to our chairs, there was a new charge in the air as we peered at everyone's glistening bodies expectantly.

"Okay," Laila said, resuming her position in her chair. "What did you discover from your little pee-blotting comparison?"

"It's true what you said," Carla nodded, proudly holding up her two samples side by side. "The pee sample had a decidedly yellow tinge to it, whereas the female ejaculation blot was clear with no staining of the tissue at all."

"What about the *smell*?" Laila said. "Did you notice a difference there too?"

"Yes," Carla nodded. "The pee had a strong urine scent, while the ejaculate had almost no smell whatsoever."

"I think you'll find once you begin to introduce this new technique with your partners, that it *tastes* a lot more pleasant too," Laila smiled. "In fact, the large quantity of glucose in your prostatic fluid that provides nutrients for sperm is actually quite *sweet*. Yet another hidden benefit of our magical feminine spring."

"Mmm," Trinity purred, already beginning to imagine trying out this new technique with her lesbian lover.

"So, are you guys ready to take this to the next level?" Laila said with a big grin on her face. "Would you like to learn how to *orgasm* at the same time you ejaculate?"

"*Fuck* yes," Carla said.

"Yes please," Piper nodded.

As we all chuckled, Laila leaned over to pick up her We-Vibe sex toy, placing it beside her on her lounge chair.

"The first thing I want you to understand is that if you continue to rely purely on *external* clitoral stimulation to orgasm, you will usually be unable to ejaculate, at least in any noticeable quantity. You'll need to change your technique in order to squirt when you come, by stimulating your G-Spot in the same manner we just learned. But *this* time, we're going to imagine erotic scenes as we stimulate ourselves and try to produce a blended orgasm."

Laila picked up her vibrator and placed it back on the floor beside her.

"Although you're welcome to use sex toys to stimulate your clitoris, for our first attempt at orgasm with ejaculation, I'm going to recommend you use your fingers only. It's important that you concentrate on the sensations you experience *everywhere* around your vulva, including the opening of your urethra, which is at the tip of your G-Spot. To get started, you may wish to close your eyes as you try to relax and focus on your feelings without getting distracted by what your seatmates are doing, or feel the pressure to come at the same time or at the same pace they do.

"On the other hand, if watching your sisters massaging their vulvas and masturbating turns you on, feel free to watch and soak up the show. Shall we get started?"

"Absolutely!" Trinity said, eager to begin.

"As before, I want you to insert the two middle fingers of your dominant hand into your pussy and gently massage your G-Spot to build up the flow of fluid to your prostate and increase the pleasurable sensations around your internal clitoris. But this time, instead of trying to *resist* the urge to orgasm, feel free to stimulate your external clit with your other hand as you feel the pleasurable sensations building up within you. When you feel yourself ready to climax, bear down like you did before and let yourself enjoy the full experience of coming in the fullest sense of the word. Let's show all the men out there that they're not the only ones who can ejaculate when they come!"

As she inserted her fingers into her vagina and began to circle her clit with her other hand, the other women slid down on their lounges, spreading their legs wide apart while they followed her lead. Unlike the last time when everybody lay fairly still while they massaged their G-Spots, this time the women moaned and squirmed in their chairs as they began to enjoy the pleasurable sensations emanating from their bodies.

Although I was eager to come after our last exercise, I was content to watch all the other women enjoying themselves as they ramped up their arousal with their two-pronged stimulation of their vulvas. It seemed everyone had a different technique for stimulating their pussies. Some of the women massaged their entire vulvas in slow up and down techniques, where others diddled their clits with rapid flapping of their fingers directly over their button. But what unified us as a group was the sight of every one of us sinking the fingers of our *other* hand into our cunts while we squeezed and stimulated our rapidly enlarging G-Spots. I'd never really spent much time feeling how my G-Spot changed in size and shape when I masturbated, but this time I could feel it growing and swelling as the pleasure began to mount and spread throughout my body.

As I felt myself getting closer and closer to orgasm, I peered around the circle becoming increasingly turned on by the sight of the other women writhing and moaning as they neared their own sexual nirvana. I was particularly focused on Claire and Piper, knowing they were the two who had expressed the strongest desire to squirt and orgasm, and as I watched their bodies progressively tighten and flush, I could feel my own climax approaching like an unstoppable freight train.

When Carla began lifting her hips off her lounge and her whole body began to tense, I stared at her pussy, excited to see her squirt for the first time while simultaneously coming. Suddenly, she emitted a loud squeal and strong jets of clear fluid squirted out of her vulva in the direction of the other women in the circle as she jerked her hips up and down in the throes of an intense full-body orgasm.

Meanwhile, a *different* kind of grunting noise was coming from Piper's direction, and I turned my head to see the familiar sex flush spreading over her pale skin, but this time her mouth gaped wide open as she trilled her clit rapidly while pressing her other hand harder into her pussy. When she finally let the floodgates open and her body began jerking wildly in the throes of climax, I smiled that she'd finally been able to turn the corner in her journey of sexual self-discovery.

As her fluids gushed out of her pussy, one by one each of the other women began to grunt and howl as they also reached the apex of their pleasure, proudly raising their hips while they squirted their love juices out over their quivering legs and the empty floor in the middle of the circle. No longer able to resist the mounting pressure inside my body, I turned to face Laila who was staring at me intently as her body began shaking and her eyes glazed over in the midst of her own powerful climax. While I watched her beautiful spray jetting out of her pussy onto the floor along with all the other women, I arched my back and growled while I locked eyes with her, coming harder than anytime I'd remembered in my life.

It seemed to take almost a full five minutes from the time the first woman popped off until the last, and when we all finished coming hard while watching each other shaking, moaning, and squirting onto the floor, we collapsed back onto our chairs, staring at the giant puddle of fluid collecting in the middle of the circle.

Venus Spring indeed, I thought, smiling over at Piper whose chest was still bobbing up and down recovering from her first incredible orgasm. *Maybe we should bottle this stuff after all. Judging by the reaction of these women, it certainly seems to be the elixir of feminine power.*

That evening, we all enjoyed hamburgers and milkshakes at Danny Meyer's famous Shake Shack in Madison Square Park, laughing and sharing stories about our craziest dates and most unusual sexual encounters. By the time we all drifted back to our hotels close to midnight, we were physically and mentally exhausted. Still, I wondered how many of the women would be able to resist the temptation to try out their newfound ejaculation skills. I had another dream about Laila, this time where she kneeled over my face while pouring her ejaculation juices into my gaping mouth. I had no idea what was in store for our last day together in the workshop, but I was determined to connect with the pretty instructor any way I could.

When we all arrived back at her apartment the following morning, we milled about for a few minutes nibbling on croissants and mini-quiches, then Laila asked us to take our seats. As we peered at each other expectantly, we squirmed in our chairs, barely able to contain our excitement.

"Did you all sleep well last night?" Laila asked.

"Like a baby," Carla said.

"It took a little while to get there," Ava said. "I was on the phone with my husband telling him about what I learned in the workshop, and we both came multiple times while I explained what he could look forward to when I returned."

"Were they nice and juicy orgasms?" Laila smiled.

"Damn right," she said. "I had to replace the towels atop the bed three times!"

"Well, I hope you guys saved a little bit for the grand finale. I thought today we might up the ante a little by *partnering* up this time. Some of you have already expressed your desire to learn how to make your female lovers squirt, and what better forum than a masturbation workshop involving ten women?"

"What if some of us aren't *lesbian*?" Piper said.

"You never know until you try," Laila said. "We're all on the spectrum somewhere. But if you're not comfortable pairing up with another woman, you're welcome to sit aside while you watch the others."

"How do we choose our partners?" Trinity said, glancing over toward Claire, who said she was attracted to women.

"I thought to make it a little more fun, we would assign the pairings by random."

She reached under her chair and pulled out a circular device that looked a bit like a double-layer roulette wheel.

"I've created this counter-rotating Wheel of Fortune spinner that will randomly select each grouping. Are you guys game to give it a try?"

"Okay..." Ava said, shifting nervously in her chair.

Laila brought the device into the middle of the circle and pointed out each of our names placed around the perimeter of the two plates. Then she spun the top plate and the pointer stopped at Carla's name. Everybody hooted and hollered while she stared at the device wondering who she'd be paired with. Laila then spun the bottom plate and it stopped on Ava's name. The group hollered even louder, realizing the two straight women would be paired up as the first couple.

As Laila continued to spin the wheels, one by one each of us got paired with another partner. Trinity got joined with Piper, I was coupled with Claire, Hailey was paired with Molly, which left the last two girls, Penelope and Willow, to join up. As we all looked at our partners excitedly, I peered over at Laila, pinching my eyebrows.

"What about *you*?" I asked. "You're the odd one out. It hardly seems fair that *we'll* be having all the fun."

"Oh, don't worry about me," she smiled. "I'll find a way to keep myself amused while you guys pair up. But if you're offering your services when you're finished with Claire, I'll be happy to join in the festivities."

"Definitely," I said, peering around the group. "We can't leave Laila unattended, can we girls?"

"No way," Trinity said. "Just make sure you save some of your juices for the *rest* of us. I've been keeping my eye on you since the start of the workshop."

"I guess you two will have to arm wrestle to see who goes first," Laila smiled.

"Or *leg* wrestle," Trinity said, winking at me.

"Okay, enough about *me*," Laila said. "This workshop is supposed to be all about you. Go ahead and enjoy yourselves and practice your new squirting skills."

"What if we've never done something like this before?" Piper said. "How do we get started?"

"Sex with a woman isn't so different from having sex with a man. Whether you choose to stimulate each other orally, digitally, or by pressing your bodies together, it's all about exploring your erogenous zones together."

"But if we're hoping to learn how to *squirt* with our partners," Hailey said. "Don't we have to massage our G-Spots while we're stimulating each other? How can we do that if we're rubbing our bodies together?"

"I'm glad you asked, Hailey," Laila smiled, reaching down toward her bag beside her chair. "Because I just happen to have a wide assortment of tools designed for the very thing."

She carried the bag to the center of the circle then one-by-one placed the oddly shaped dildos on a towel on the floor. One was made of clear glass and shaped in the form of an S, with a glass ball on each end. Another one was made of stainless steel and curved in a C-shape with two different-sized bulbs at each end. Yet another was made of silicone and shaped like a curved L with different-shaped protrusions at each end. By the time she'd finished laying out the entire collection, our eyes bulged in shock, wondering how to use them.

"Now you don't have to actually use any of these if you don't want to," Laila said, noticing the look of terror on many of the women's faces. "As we've seen, sometimes the most satisfying way to stimulate the G-spot is with our fingers. There's something to be said for actually *feeling* your partner's physical response as she becomes aroused."

"How exactly do we use some of those things?" Ava said, peering at the S-shaped dildo curiously.

"I'm going to let you guys figure that out for yourself," Laila said. "Each of them is curved in a different way, so you'll just have to experiment with adjusting your body positions until you find one that works for both of you."

"Where do you want us to set up?" Carla said. "It might be hard for both of us to fit on our individual chairs."

"That depends on the manner in which you choose to engage. If you choose to stimulate your partner orally or with your fingers, you might find the curvature of the chairs is ideal for stimulating her clitoris and G-Spot. On the other hand, if you prefer to rub your bodies together, feel free to spread out some towels on the floor and get down and dirty."

Everybody paused for a moment while we peered at Laila, unsure how to proceed.

"Well, what are you waiting for?" Laila said. "We haven't got all day! Remember today's session ends at 2 p.m. to give you enough time to catch your flights back home."

Claire and I peered hesitatingly at one another, then I grabbed her hand, leading her to the side of the living room where I laid each of our towels end-over-end. Trinity was next to approach Piper, crawling up the end of her lounge chair like a prowling cat. Carla picked up one of the double-dildos lying on the floor then kneeled on top of Ava's lap, licking her lips excitedly. By the time each of us had joined up with our appointed partners, I noticed all of the girls melting into each other's arms.

"You don't want to try using one of the *toys*?" Claire said to me as we squatted on the floor.

"Since this is your first time with a woman," I said, I'd rather feel your skin without the help of any sex aid. "There are so many different ways to please a woman."

"So you've done this before?" she said.

"Maybe once or twice," I smiled.

As I leaned in to kiss her, I cupped her breast in my hand, pinching her nipple softly between my fingers. She gasped into my mouth and pressed her mound against the side of my hips. While I watched her chest rising and falling in excitement, I slid my hand down her quivering tummy toward the cleft in her legs, pausing to brush my fingers through her soft muff. It was already sprinkled with dew, and I rubbed her moisture teasingly over her bush like a hairdresser massaging conditioner into her scalp. She spread her legs apart a few inches and raised her hips, eager for me to go lower.

When I rolled my hand over her vulva, I was surprised how wet she already was, and I tickled the inside of her lips by running my fingers up and down the length of her folds, purposefully avoiding her swelling button. Even though I knew she was desperate for me to touch her clit, I was mindful of Laila's earlier instruction to focus on massaging her G-Spot first if I wanted to make her squirt, then move to her clit when she was getting close to orgasm.

When I slipped my two middle fingers into her hole, she shuddered, rolling her tongue around the inside of my mouth, encouraging me to explore further. I pressed my fingers as deep as I could into her cavern, pressing my palm hard against her cunt, and she groaned deeply. Then I curled my fingers slowly upward, pressing them toward the roof of her vagina, feeling the soft tissue near the rear of her canal.

It was fascinating for me to examine another woman's G-Spot clinically for the first time, and as I pulled my fingers closer toward the front of her pussy, I could feel the egg-shaped protrusion swelling and hardening until I reached the horizontal ridges about two joints inside.

Holy smoke, I thought to myself. *It's true that we're all built the same way and every woman is equipped with the same tools to ejaculate.* Up until two days ago, I had no idea that the G-Spot was actually a water-filled bulb surrounding the urethra that we could use to express and squirt at will.

As I continued massaging Claire's bump, her breathing became more ragged and she began to tighten her body, lifting her hips off the floor. I sensed she was close to coming, and paused for a moment, looking at her pretty face.

"What are you stopping for?" she said, peering at me beseechingly. "I was just about to come!"

"I know," I smiled. "But I want to see you *squirt* when you climax. We're supposed to take it slow, remember? Besides, I want to *taste* you when you come this first time."

Claire's eyes suddenly widened when she realized what I was suggesting, and as I shimmied my body lower down her figure, I peered up at her with a wicked smile.

I'm gonna show this girl how a woman properly gets licked, I thought to myself.

When I positioned my face between her legs, she spread her knees apart and I stared at her vulva for a moment, watching her natural juices dripping down her perineum and over the crack of her ass.

The female prostate isn't the only part of a woman's body that knows how to lubricate the pussy, I smiled.

I lowered my face to her vulva, lapping my tongue against the sides of her slippery lips, then I thrust it inside her hole, curving it up toward her swelling bump.

I have got to do this more often, I thought, feeling the familiar ridges of her G-Spot. *Now that I know how to properly stimulate this organ, this is way too much fun to pass up.*

As I rolled my tongue from side to side over her bulb, Claire mashed her pussy against my face, reveling in her first lesbian experience with oral sex. I could feel her buttocks tightening and her thigh muscles clenching, and knew that she was on the verge of coming once again, and I pulled out, smiling at her as drips of lubrication ran down my chin.

"Oh God, Jade," she pleaded. "I need to come so bad. Don't stop. I want to cum all over your face."

"Okay," I said. "But remember what Laila said. When you feel yourself on the brink of orgasm, don't resist the urge to pee. Remember to bear down and push out at the moment of climax. Give me a warning so I can pull out my fingers and allow you to eject all your fluid."

"Oh, I'll give you a *warning* alright," she panted.

"Okay," I nodded. "I'm going to stimulate you on both sides now. When you're ready, just let it all go."

"I will," Claire nodded excitedly.

When I lowered my face to her pussy, this time I slipped two fingers inside her while I encircled her burning clit between my lips. As I began to bathe her bulb with my undulating tongue, I peered up for a moment to watch the other women around the room. Piper was sitting atop Trinity's face, writhing in ecstasy as the cute African-American girl massaged her G-Spot with her right hand. Hailey and Molly were lying on the floor in a sixty-nine position, eating each other's pussies with their hands buried knuckle-deep in their respective cunts. Ava and Carla had their asses pressed together, rocking their pussies as the curved glass dildo glistening between their flapping vulvas.

Looks like they figured out the right position to use that S-shaped dildo after all, I smiled to myself.

As I peered around the room listening to all the woman groaning and wailing on the verge of orgasm, I suddenly felt Claire's pussy tenting toward the far end, and I peered up at her.

"Yes, Jade," she panted. "I'm going to come now. Fuck, I'm going to cum so hard. I'm going to bathe your beautiful face with my juices."

As she raised her hips higher off the floor and straightened her legs at the edge of climax, I pulled my fingers out of her and watched her perineal muscles pulsing as she squirted her juices all over my blinking face. While she screamed and hollered in orgasmic delight, I smiled with a radiant glow knowing that her first climax with another woman was a full-body experience, where she'd experienced the true pinnacle of pleasure.

As I held her quaking body, letting her juices spray all over my bare tits, I peered around the room, noticing all the other women squirting just as strongly in the full embrace of their partners.

God damn, I thought. *Those Eastern religions had it right. This female ejaculation thing truly is a spiritual experience.*

8

When the last of the couples had finished ejaculating together, we all lay exhausted in a disheveled heap on the floor, panting and hugging each other happily. But I knew there was still almost two hours left in our workshop and after we all had a quick helping of pizza delivered to the door, we returned to our lounge seats to discuss our experience.

"So, what do you think?" Laila asked with a knowing smile. "Was it as much fun to ejaculate with a partner as it was by self-stimulation?"

"Much more!" Piper interjected, smiling at her partner, Trinity.

"I had no idea having sex with a woman could be as rewarding as with a man," Ava said.

"With the right instruments, *anything* is possible," Laila winked, peering down at their still-glistening glass dildo.

"How about you, Claire?" How did you find your first introduction to girl-on-girl sex?"

"Oh my God," she sighed, peering over at me. "It was even better than I imagined. My only regret is that I won't have even more time in the workshop to spread the love around."

"Something tells me you won't find it so awkward finding new lesbian lovers when you get back home after all this."

Everybody laughed and clapped once again to give recognition for the collective achievement we'd all made in the short time we'd been together.

"We still have a little bit of time left in the workshop," Laila said. "Do you have any questions or would you like to discuss some new techniques for stimulating your partners when you get back home?

"Screw *that*," Trinity said. "We all want to see you get down and dirty now, don't we girls? I'm pretty sure every one of us has been dreaming about fucking you ever since you showed us how to squirt."

"Well, I'm not sure I can accommodate everyone at the same time," Laila smiled. But I might have enough time for one more pairing. How do you want to go about doing this?"

"What about using your magic wheel?" Carla said. "Can you give it one last spin to see which of us gets the chance to make love to you?"

"I suppose that might work," Laila said, lifting the device back onto her lap. "But there's two different wheels with different names on each layer. I'll have to spin it twice to see who wins."

"Go for it," Trinity said, itching at her chance to get together with the sexy instructor.

Laila spun the top plate and when the needle stopped it pointed toward me.

"Woo-hoo!" everybody cheered, peering at me with broad smiles.

"I'm not quite there yet," I said, waiting to see who would be selected when she spun the bottom wheel.

When it finished turning, the needle pointed toward Trinity.

"Hmm," Laila said, feigning dismay. "We seem to have a quandary as to which of you should have your turn."

"Maybe we should have a squirt-off," Trinity joked. "To see who can ejaculate the furthest."

"Or use a bowl to see who can produce the most fluid," I winked.

"Although I'm sure that might be interesting to watch, remember how I said earlier that the best way to ensure a satisfying ejaculation experience is to relax and not feel any pressure to perform? I think we're going to have to find *another* way to decide who I'll pair up with."

Laila removed all the other women's names from the top wheel except mine, then she lifted the name tag for Trinity off the bottom plate and placed it next to mine.

"Are you guys ready?" she said, looking up at the two of us with her hand poised on the needle.

"Are you *kidding* me?" Trinity said. "I'm about to pop off just watching you spinning the wheel! Get on with it. You're killing me here!"

Laila flicked the wheel hard with her finger and all of us watched the needle spinning for a few long moments until it finally stopped against my name.

"Woo-hoo," everybody yelled, eager to get on with the show.

"Sorry, hun," I said, cocking my head toward Trinity. "But someone's gotta do the dirty deed."

"You better make it good, bitch," she smiled back at me.

"Where do you want to do this?" I said, looking at Laila.

"Well, since all of you wanted a piece of me, I suppose it's only fair to do it in the middle of the circle, where everyone can watch."

"Works for me," I said. "Do you have a preference for how we do this? *With* toys or without?"

"Actually, in this case," Laila purred. "I think I'd like to try it *with*. I have a special toy that I like to use for these special occasions."

"Oh?" I said, raising an inquisitive eyebrow.

She reached down into her bag and pulled out a polished wood S-shaped dildo with a carved ball on one end.

"This is called the Noblesse Seduction G-Spot Dildo," Laila said. "It's carved out of real walnut and it has a special place in my heart."

"Not to mention a few *other* special places, I'm sure," I smiled. "I've never used one with that shape before. Is there a special position we need to be in to make it work?"

"There are actually quite a few different positions we could use to enjoy it," she said. "But I had one particular one in mind for you. Why don't you lie down on the floor on your tummy?"

"Um, okay..." I said, happy to assume the submissive position for a change.

As I lay down on the floor with all the other girls perched on the ends of their chairs ready to watch the action, Laila reached into her bag and pulled out a small tube.

"I'm going to lube this up a bit first, to make sure no one gets hurt–"

"I don't think you're going to need much of that," I purred, tilting my glistening pussy up for her to see. "I'm pretty damn wet already just thinking about what you're going to do with that thing."

Laila placed a small dollop of lube on both ends of the gleaming tool, then she kneeled down with her thighs straddling my ass and inserted the thick end in her pussy. Then she twisted the dildo until the curved ball was pointing downward and positioned it against my flaring lips.

"Uhnnn," I groaned, feeling it rubbing against my opening. "I like the feel of that. It's nice and smooth."

"And *hard*," Laila said, pressing her hips forward and inserting the device into my pussy.

I could feel the curved ball pressing down against the roof of my vagina, and as she began to rock her hips toward my ass, it slid over my bulging G-Spot, stimulating me unlike any dildo I'd felt before.

"Fuck yes," I purred. "Fuck me with your pretty brown dildo, Laila. Massage my G-Spot with your big curved dick. I like it when you fuck me from behind."

"Yeah?" Laila said, taunting me. "Do you like it as much as a man's cock? Do you like it this hard?"

"It's harder than any *man* I've known, that's for sure," I purred. "But knowing it's attached to a pretty girl makes it a lot more exciting for me."

"You like getting fucked by girls?"

"Sometimes," I grunted as she slapped her mound harder against my ass. This was the first time during the workshop where I'd heard her talk dirty, and it was turning me on like crazy. "Especially one who knows what she's doing."

"Are you ready to come with me?" she panted, rocking her hips more forcefully against my ass.

"God, yes," I growled.

I could feel my G-Spot swelling as she continued massaging it with the flared bulb of the dildo, and as I began to feel shoots of electricity running up and down my thighs, I reached behind me, digging my nails into the side of her hips, pulling her harder toward me.

"I'm going to squirt all over your pretty pussy when I come," I groaned. "I almost there. Oh *fuckkkk...*"

Suddenly, Laila pulled out of me and tossed the wooden dildo to the side as we both howled at the top of our lungs, spraying our juices all over each other while the rest of the girls gaped at us with wide eyes. As Laila started spraying over my quivering ass, I tilted my hips up toward her, squirting my juices against her flapping cunt like a firehose. When we finally collapsed onto one another in a giant puddle of clear fluid on the floor, the entire room erupted in an enormous round of applause.

Talk about a 'hands-on' workshop, I smiled to myself, panting heavily beside Laila. *This Fountain of Venus seminar has taken the concept to an entirely new level.*

VICTORIA RUSH

PEEP
SHOW
EROTIC ADVENTURE

1

After going over a week without any type of intimate contact, I was feeling especially horny today. In such circumstances, I'd normally go online to find an outlet to relieve my built-up sexual tension. But lately, I'd been finding that internet porn wasn't doing it for me. Sure, the girls were always hot and sexy and I could generally find something new and interesting to get me in the mood. But it all seemed so impersonal, so *manufactured*. Even my favorite lesbian webcam site had become a disappointment, with viewers swiping from one partner to the next, often right in the middle of a hot-and-heavy session.

I needed some real flesh and blood contact, or at least be able to *see* someone live. But I didn't just want to see and hear her, I wanted to smell her, feel her, *taste* her. Somebody who wouldn't exit the scene at the first sign of boredom, or as soon as she got her rocks off. I wanted to be with someone I could take my time with and enjoy the experience on my own terms. And *Tinder* was out of the question, since I didn't have the time or the energy to vet the candidates, nor string along the ones whose profile never seemed to align with their real personas.

After trolling through the usual online sources, I decided to try something new. I clicked on the latest issue of the Windy City Times, Chicago's long-time LGBTQ newspaper. At least here, I knew I'd be able to find authentic lesbian, bi, and trans girls. Among the litany of gay bar postings, I found an unusual listing in the classified section. Under the headline *Nude Casting Call* was an ad for open auditions at the local theater company. Intrigued, I clicked on the Details tab and began to read the full description:

> *The Bijou Theater is looking for uninhibited people who are interested in staging solo performances in the nude. With a king-size bed as your primary prop, your goal is to arouse and titillate a live audience using only your body and your wild imagination. There will be boys-only, girls-only, and mixed couples events, so you can cater your performance to your own sexual preference or mix it up as you see fit.*
>
> *A winner will be chosen after each audition based on audience response, with the winners moving on to regional semi-finals and finals. The Grand Prize winner will win an all-expense-paid vacation for two to the Desire Riviera Maya Resort in Puerto Morales, Mexico. Exhibitionists and voyeurs alike are encouraged to attend. Come one, come all!*

Holy shit, I thought, suddenly aware of the growing dampness in my panties. The idea of watching someone perform an erotic routine for a live audience definitely got my motor running. This wasn't some sleazy dive bar or strip club where the girls performed nude dances in front of a bunch of leering men. This was a legitimate theater where amateur performers volunteered to display their naked bodies to a group of of anonymous strangers in a darkened auditorium. And I could *choose* the target audience–no sweaty old men, no creepy lap dances, no private rooms where the girls were paid for private favors. I could just sit back and enjoy the show in the privacy of my own darkened alcove.

But what exactly did they mean by *solo performances*? Just how far did these performances go? Did they touch their bodies only superficially, simulating sex acts like a typical stripper? Or did they caress themselves in their most private regions, with the purpose of genuinely getting themselves and their onlookers off? The presence of a bed on the stage suggested it would be more than just a typical erotic dance. And how much audience participation would there be in the production? Were spectators allowed to actively stimulate *themselves* in the dark while they watched the performers on stage?

The more I thought about it, the more turned on I got imagining how exciting it would be to take in a live performance. Hell, if the conditions were right and the security was good enough, I might be tempted to give it a go myself. But first, I needed to check it out from the protection of the viewing gallery. At least there I'd be able to get my rocks off watching somebody else in the relative safety of a darkened auditorium. We could *both* take our time to ramp up our desire, knowing the only consideration was maximizing everyone's viewing pleasure and satisfaction.

I clicked on the Calendar tab and noticed a selection of dates highlighted in different colors and markings. Pink shading signified ladies-only nights, blue was men-only, and green was open to both sexes. A downward-sloping diagonal line through the box meant the show was sold out for new audience members, and an upward-sloping line meant auditions had been fully booked for that day's event. Scrolling through the pink-shaded boxes, I saw that the next three week's events were X'd out, indicating there was no room for either performers or attendees. The next available ladies night only had one line crossed through it, so I click on the date and booked a ticket immediately.

As I leaned back in my chair, imagining myself watching a pretty girl caressing herself on stage, I pulled down my panties and began rubbing my inflamed clit.

This is going to be interesting, I thought.

When the audition night finally arrived, I went to the theater and presented my online ticket to the attendant. A few other girls were waiting along with me behind the turnstiles, and after security checked our driver's licenses to verify our age and sex, they handed each of us a small bag and we entered the darkened theater, locating the closest seats to the stage. I peered in the bag and saw that it contained two items: a disposable plastic seat cover and a small box of Kleenex tissues. I smiled knowingly, then carefully spread the latex cover over the top of my chair. When I sat down and peered around me, I noticed that the room was only half full. Most of the seats were occupied by lone viewers with at least two or three open spaces separating them. I nodded, happy with the way the theater had set everything up for the maximum privacy and comfort of the spectators.

But I noticed there was also a sprinkling of same-sex couples strewn about the theater who were giggling and making out in their private cubbyholes. There was just enough light to notice that everybody was female, but not enough to establish their identities. Suddenly, the lights dimmed and a middle-aged woman walked out onto the middle of the stage under a bright spotlight. I recognized a familiar shape in the shadows behind her, and my heart began to flutter knowing that a nude performer would soon be lying on the bed, giving us a show to remember.

"Good evening, *ladies and voyeurs*!" she announced, holding the mic to her mouth. "Are you ready for some uniquely stimulating entertainment?"

A few people whooped and hollered, while others clapped excitedly. I wondered how many in the audience were 'regulars' who were there mostly to pass judgement on the performances, versus the first-timers like me who were there mostly for the intrigue and the stimulation.

"Those of you who've been here before already know the rules," the woman continued. "But allow me to educate the rest of the crowd to ensure the safety and satisfaction of all participants."

The buzz in the theater suddenly subsided as everyone allowed the MC to finish her briefing.

"Audience members are permitted to encourage the performers with verbal feedback, but we ask that you keep it upbeat at all times. Many of our performers are first-time auditioners, and we wish to provide them with a positive environment to express themselves openly. At the end of each performance we'll ask for your collective feedback to help us judge who should be moved on to the next stage of the competition. No booing or cat-calls–only clapping or cheering to reflect the degree to which you felt entertained. As always, we ask you to remain in your seats until the end of each performance unless you need to use the restrooms in the rear of the theater. For the safety and privacy of every performer, no one will be permitted to approach the stage at any time. Anyone breaking these rules will be promptly escorted out of the theater."

The woman paused for a moment to make sure everyone understood the ground rules. I nodded my head, beginning to appreciate the level of safety and security afforded the performers and audience members alike.

"Any questions?" the MC asked.

The room filled with silence, as everybody anticipated the next move.

"All right then," she said, swinging her arm to the side of the stage where the spotlight focused on a closed curtain hanging in the wings. "Let the show begin!"

As she receded to the opposite side of the stage, the curtain parted and a young woman looking to be in her late teens or early twenties tiptoed out onto the stage wearing a thin bathrobe. She glanced shyly toward the darkened auditorium, then walked purposefully across the stage to the king-size bed, now brightly illuminated under two criss-crossing spotlights. When she reached the edge of the bed, she paused for a moment then pulled her robe off her body and hung it on the side of the headboard, quickly slipping under the linen sheets.

I was able to catch just enough of her naked body to see that she had a petite frame and an agile figure. Her ass was firm and round, and her legs tapered with the grace of a short-track sprinter. I wondered if she might have been a college athlete. Because she'd turned her body away from the audience as she got under the covers, I wasn't able to see much of her upper body, which she'd kept carefully covered with crossed arms. But her face was young and pretty, with the plump skin, full eyebrows, and the unruffled hairstyle of a carefree adolescent.

My pussy twitched as I watched her climb into the bed, pulling the sheets high up under her neck with two hands. I smiled at how shy she was and wondered what had prompted her to participate in such an event if she felt so nervous about displaying her body. Maybe it had been a dare between her and her friends, or maybe her boy or girlfriend had put her up to it, or maybe she just wanted to experience the excitement of being naked in a room full of strangers. Either way, I found the whole premise highly stimulating, and I squirmed in my seat as I found myself getting more turned on by the moment.

I'd decided to wear a mid-length skirt and button-up blouse with no underwear underneath to provide maximum freedom of movement in the event I had the opportunity to touch myself. As I watched the girl lower one hand down the front of her abdomen under the thin sheet, my legs began to spread apart unconsciously. She still held the covers tightly under her chin with one hand, but the flimsy fabric meandering like a snake left little doubt what she was doing. At first, she teasingly cupped one of her breasts with her free hand, pinching the nipple with her fingers as her eyes darted tentatively around the darkened theater. I could tell she was nervous and excited at the same time, and I was happy she couldn't see any of our faces to embolden her actions.

Mmm, a few people in the audience hummed, encouraging her to continue. The girl smiled then inched her hand lower down her abdomen. When it reached the top of her hips, I saw her fingers probe the area near the base of her mound, and her face twitched when she found her sensitive spot. As she began to circle her fingers over her love button, my own fingers began to inch under my skirt toward my tingling gland. There was something incredibly sexy about watching a young girl touch herself under the covers, knowing that everyone's eyes in the room were glued on her.

With the murmurs from the audience turning from hums of approval to gentle moans, the girl slowly began to spread her legs, as the movement of her hand between her legs started to speed up. I could see her chest beginning to rise and fall as her desire began to mount, and she tried to keep a straight face as her lips puckered and her eyelashes batted intermittently while a gentle flush began to spread over her cheeks.

"Show us more!" one of the couples in the corner yelled.

The girl stopped moving for a moment, temporarily taken aback by the intrusion, then she slowly lowered the cover down to the base of her hips. Her tits were small but perky, resting high on her chest in a sexy crescent shape, with large areolas and dark nubs. She lifted her other hand from under the sheet and cupped both of them, pinching her hardening nipples between her fingers.

"*Yes,*" somebody purred a few rows in front of me.

Emboldened by the audience's reaction, the girl soon traced one hand back down under the sheets and resumed stimulating her pussy. As I watched the sheets tenting and puffing from the action of her hand, I slipped my own hand under my skirt and began mimicking her movement, stroking and caressing my little man-in-the-boat. I didn't know exactly why, but I found the experience of watching a live girl touching herself in a darkened theater much more arousing than watching somebody masturbate online.

I was dying to see more of her body and just when I was about to encourage her to pull the sheets down a little further, someone else in the audience beat me to it.

"Let us see your pretty pussy," someone called from the back of the theater.

The girl paused for a moment, unsure how much she wanted to reveal. Then she drew her legs back together and pulled the covers down over her knees. I could see her hairy muff sitting on top of her mound, glistening from the juices she'd been spreading over the area with her free hand. She began to separate her legs, then suddenly stopped, not ready to reveal her most private areas to a room full of strangers. But her heaving chest indicated that she was still turned on and desperate to touch herself.

Suddenly, she flipped over onto her stomach, placing both of her hands under her crotch with her legs tightly closed. As I watched her buttocks flexing and her hips pressing rhythmically down onto the mattress, it became apparent to everyone watching exactly what she was doing with her hands. While her hips began to flop up and down on the mattress, her mouth spread open as a flush rolled over her face.

Fuck, I murmured to myself, watching her jill herself under her stomach. *That is so hot!*

Seeing her masturbating so demurely with her pretty ass and back toward us was somehow even more of a turn-on than watching her close-up. I thrust my fingers inside my cunt and began fucking myself more vigorously, imagining myself straddling her with a strap-on dildo.

God, how I'd like a piece of that pretty ass.

"Spread your legs further apart!" someone called from the other side of the theater.

As if on cue, the girl began to spread her thighs until they were separated about thirty degrees apart. I could now see her fingers moving rapidly between her cleft with the underside of her glistening slit poking tantalizingly between her pink globes.

As the sound of impassioned sighs and moans began to spread around the theater, I glanced around me and noticed the telltale sign of movement in the adjacent seats. Many of the girls in my row had their legs spread wide apart as they stroked their pussies while they watched the pretty girl on the stage grow increasingly excited. I glanced at one of the couples in the corner and saw that one girl had her leg raised over the armrest while her partner rammed her fingers into her snatch as she kissed her passionately.

Suddenly, the girl on the stage began to moan more loudly as she angled her ass upwards, spreading her knees further apart. We could now see her entire glistening vulva, highlighted by the twin spotlights shining on her ass, from her pretty pink pucker down past her slit all the way to her hairy muff. As she sped up the movement of her right hand circling her clit, she reached further down between her legs with her other hand and inserted two fingers inside her hole.

She was now unashamedly fucking herself with two hands for the entire theater to see, with no further impediments, or hint of shyness. I could hear the sound of other fingers sloshing in and out of pussies all around me as other horny audience members rammed themselves in sympathy with the girl on the stage. Within seconds, a crimson flush spread over the girl's cheeks and her buttocks began to tremble. As her knees began to wobble from side to side, she squealed like an injured animal, caught up in the throes of a powerful orgasm.

Watching her come in full view of the surrounding audience was more than I could bear, and I arched my back, clamping down hard over my fingers, spraying my pent-up juices all over the metal back of the seat in front of me. As soft gasps and groans emanated from every corner of the theater, the turned-on crowd released their own pent-up pleasure in tandem with the pretty co-ed. I glanced over at the lesbian couple in the corner and saw the girl with her leg over the armrest convulsing in pleasure as her partner rammed her fist into her while they both watched the stage, transfixed by the erotic performance.

When the pretty coed finally stopped shaking, she pulled the sheets back up over her body and the stage darkened, as the spotlight shifted to the curtains on the opposite side of the rostrum. The MC walked back out onto the platform, holding a small device in her hand.

"What did you guys think?" she asked, pointing her smartphone out to the crowd. "Was that worthy of an encore appearance?"

"Woo-hoo!" some audience members hollered.

I noticed a needle swing clockwise on the decibel-reading app.

"Let's give the young lady a *proper* round of applause," the MC hollered. "Show her how much you all *really* enjoyed the performance!"

The crowd erupted in applause and cheering, demonstrating their appreciation and satisfaction with the performance. I noticed the needle swing about sixty percent of the way around the circle, and the MC turned the device around to register the results.

"Let's take a little breather while we give our next performer a few minutes to prepare," she nodded. "But compose yourselves, because the next performer is a crowd favorite!"

As the woman strolled back into the shadows, a group of stagehands began remaking the now empty bed with a fresh set of linens.

I wish they'd offer us a similar turndown service, I thought as I wiped the back of the seat in front of me with one of the napkins provided in my care package. *Because if that girl only justifies a rating of sixty percent, I'm going to need some fresh towels before this evening is over.*

2

———————

s I watched the next three performers, I grew increasing
aroused by the sexually charged atmosphere in the room.
At the end of the evening, the prize for best performance
was awarded to an older, more seasoned actor, but I couldn't get the
image of the young coed shaking quietly on the bed out of my head.
There was something about her self-effacing nature that turned me
on like no one I'd seen in a long time. I went home that night and had
three more powerful orgasms imagining it was *me* planted between
her thighs instead of her hand.

But I had far from satisfied my thirst for this intoxicating production. I immediately booked the next available ladies-night audition
then spent the next two weeks practicing my own erotic act in front of
my full-length dressing mirror. I wasn't quite ready to go on stage and
bare my soul for a room full of strangers, but I found the idea incredibly stimulating, and every time I thought about it I came harder than
I had in a long time.

When the night of the next auditions rolled around, I was already
soaking wet by the time I entered the building's lobby. I looked
around me and saw a familiar collection of singles and couples
waiting to be admitted, but there was one pretty girl at the end of the

line who caught my eye. Wearing black tights and a loose-fitting, cropped t-shirt, her tight ass and plump breasts barely concealed by her open midriff got me even more excited. As I stole glances at her sexy body, dribbles of lubrication began streaming down the inside of my thighs under my pantyless skirt.

Everybody seemed too nervous to strike up a conversation while we waited to go inside, embarrassed by the obvious reason for our attendance at the event. Like a bunch of perverts in a peep-show theater, we just wanted to hide in the shadows while we silently got our rocks off watching the action on the stage. I turned my body sideways, trying to distract the girl's attention from the river cascading down my legs while pretending to fish around for something in my purse.

After presenting my ID to the security guard, I hurried through the turnstiles and walked into the darkened theater. It was more full than last time, but I found a secluded seat about fifteen rows back from the stage. As the lights began to dim in preparation for the main event, another viewer side-stepped her way into my row and stopped a few seats away from me. I looked up and noticed that it was the girl from the lobby.

"Is this spot taken?" she asked, pointing to the seat next to mine.

I glanced around the theater noticing a few other open spots slightly further back, but for some reason I didn't mind having my personal space encroached upon this time.

"Um, no," I said, motioning to the open seat. "Help yourself."

The girl opened her care package and spread the disposable seat cover over the chair then sat down, placing her purse on the opposite armrest. It felt a bit uncomfortable having someone sitting so close to me, but my rapidly beating heart belied my true feelings.

"It's a little busier than usual tonight," she said, spreading her legs apart to make herself more comfortable.

I glanced down between her thighs and noticed a dark patch in the crotch of her tight pants. Apparently more than one of us had gotten herself worked up in preparation for the night's festivities.

"Oh?" I said, pretending to be disinterested. "I wouldn't know–it's only my second time coming to this event."

"This must be my seventh or eighth time at least" she said, not letting me off the hook so easily. "When were you last here?"

"Two weeks ago, on the last ladies' night."

"I remember that one," she nodded. "That was the one with the cute college girl who needed a little extra encouragement to show her body."

"Yes."

"She was a hot little thing, wasn't she? But I thought she got cheated out the most erotic performance of the night. I guess the more skin they show and the more outrageous the performance, the higher the scores they receive from the hardcore regulars."

"Mmm," I nodded.

"Do you prefer girls?" she asked. "I mean to *watch*?"

"I guess so," I said. "I find them sexier, but I also feel safer around other women. I don't really want to be surrounded by a bunch of lecherous dudes jerking off a few feet away from me."

"I know what you mean," she said, lifting her sneakers off the floor, one at a time. "At least the theater keeps the place pretty clean. They probably have to send a hazmat team in here after each show."

I shuffled my ass on the latex seat beneath me and smiled.

"Thank heavens for these sanitary seat covers," I said. "I can't imagine sitting anywhere in this place without them."

"And the *napkins*," the girl said, waving one in front of her crotch. "You can never have enough of these things once the action gets hot and heavy."

I was about to introduce myself when the lights in the theater dimmed and the MC walked out onto the stage. But I hardly heard anything she said while I ogled the girl's body next to me. As she leaned back in her seat to get more comfortable, her cutoff shirt slid further up her abdomen, showing the bottom of her fleshy tits. The sensuous curve of her mounds taunted me in the shadows, and I squeezed my thighs together trying to quell my itchy clit.

When I looked back up toward the stage, a sexy blonde girl was kneeling on the bed facing the crowd with her thighs spread about two feet apart. She was wearing a full-length body suit with holes cut out over the tops of her breasts and crotch to reveal her private parts. The effect magnified the size of her breasts, highlighting her pink nipples poking sensuously out of the thin fabric. But it was the effect on her *lower* body than really got my juices flowing. The only part of her crotch that was showing was her bright pink vulva, shining like the petals of a flower surrounded by the darkened landscape of her tight-fitting leotard.

"*Fuck*, that's hot," the girl next to me hissed, spreading her legs wider apart.

The girl on the stage suddenly swung around with her back to the audience, straightening her legs to her sides as she slowly lowered her crotch to the surface of the bed, performing a perfect split. Then she tilted her ass slightly upward, revealing her pink slit shining like a conch shell on a barren beach. As I squirmed in my chair, mesmerized by the girl's erotic performance, my legs began to spread apart with a mind of their own.

"Do you mind if I make myself more comfortable?" the girl sitting next to me said, pulling her black tights down over her knees. "I'm feeling the need to give my pussy a little breathing room of its own."

"By all means," I said, now fully on board with the idea of having a partner I could enjoy the show with.

She pulled her tights down over her ankles, draping them over the back of the seat next to her, then placed her ankles on the seat rests in front of her, bending her knees as she tilted her hips forward. I could see her bald mound and protruding nub glistening in the reflected light from the stage as my own pussy began to dribble onto the seat cushion beneath me.

Some movement on the stage caught my attention, and I looked up to see the blond girl flip over like a breakdancer, slicing her legs open into a wide scissor shape. With one foot pointed tantalizingly toward the audience and the other nestled under her shoulder, she was practically *begging* us touch her glistening gash.

"*Damn*," my seatmate groaned, now unashamedly rubbing her

snatch with her right hand. "I'd sit on that pretty pussy and grind my cunt against hers *any* time."

I slid my hand under my skirt and began to circle my burning nub, thinking exactly the same thing. It had been a while since I'd felt another woman's wet pussy against my own, and I fantasized about kneeling between the blond girl's legs and lowering my hips onto hers.

"Mmm," I nodded as my body began to radiate in pleasure.

Hearing the sound of soft moans and sighs emanating from the amphitheater, the girl suddenly pulled her legs together and pointed them straight up in the air. The curl of her feet and the gentle musculature of her thighs as she flexed her legs reminded me of a ballerina, and I wondered if she might be a professional dancer. But it was the exposed folds of flesh between her tight buttocks that I was focused on at this particular moment. As they spilled out of her torn bodysuit like an open clam shell, my mouth watered imagining myself sucking her pretty pussy while she went through her poses.

Just when I thought it couldn't get any hotter, she lowered her legs into another perfect split framing her face as she peered out into the audience. She began to curl her body forward as she smiled at her hidden admirers while she rolled her fingers over her puffy petals.

"Fuck, yes," the girl next to me hissed, spreading her legs further apart until her knee touched my elbow resting beside her on my armrest. "That is one gorgeous pussy. I'd water that flower any day."

As my seatmate tilted her head back onto the backrest and sped up the motion of her hand between her pussy, the girl on the stage reached under the covers and lifted a strange-looking device into the air above her splayed body. It looked like a type of dildo, but not like anything I'd seen before. This one had deep diagonal grooves in the shaft, making it look like an oversize plastic screw. She tapped a button on the base of the unit it suddenly began to gyrate in a circular flapping motion. Then she held the tip against the opening of her pink slit and slowly sunk the rotating dildo into her hole.

While the crowd watched in mesmerized silence, she began to

shake her hips back and forth as she grasped her ankles with outstretched arms. The whole scene looked surreal–like she was some kind of bendable doll with an animatronic dildo flopping around in her snatch as she smiled out into the audience. But the flush spreading across her face quickly reminded me this was no act, as her mouth began to gape open from the pleasure that was spreading inside her body.

Suddenly the girl next to me turned to look for something in her purse and she pulled out a large dildo. I recognized the shape of it instantly, with its penis-shaped tip and protruding rabbit ears on the shaft. She tapped two buttons on the base, then plunged it deep inside her sopping pussy, ramming it in and out of her sloshing hole. Having one just like it at home, I knew exactly what was happening as she held it tightly against her with two hands. While circulating beads around the perimeter of the shaft stimulated the walls of her tunnel, the articulated tip rotated around in circles caressing her G-spot as the flapping external appendages straddled the shaft of her clit, providing intense external stimulation.

As I peered back and forth between the contortionist on the stage and the sexy girl ramming her pussy next to me, I plunged the fingers of my right hand into my hole and began groaning along with the rest of the audience. When the girl on the stage arched her back off the surface of the bed, bringing her face closer to the gyrating instrument flapping wildly inside her pussy, I could feel my own pleasure rising toward its inevitable denouement as my body began to tense up.

Suddenly, her buttocks and thighs began shaking as her head jerked forward and back in unison with the writhing serpent between her legs. I saw her sex flush spread up her long slender neck then all over her face as she grimaced in climactic pleasure.

"Oh my *God*," the girl next to me groaned as her own body began shaking in convulsive spasms with the pulsing vibrator buzzing between her legs. Seeing both girls coming so strongly soon put me over the edge as I slipped my knuckles past the opening to my pussy while I pounded my G-spot with my fist, grunting in a series of powerful contractions.

"Uhn, uhn, uhn," I groaned, feeling the pressure building inside my tunnel.

Just before I finished coming, I pulled my hand out of my hole, jetting my juices forward like a garden hose. The intense spray bounced off the back of the chair in front of me, sprinkling droplets all over the front of my seatmate's body. She looked up at me and mouthed the words *fuck me*, taken aback in surprise. I leaned over and kissed her passionately, cupping her quivering tits as she pressed the still-vibrating dildo hard against her vulva. When we both finally stopped coming, we flopped back against our seat rests, panting in exhaustion from the intense workout we'd both experienced watching the sexy scene on the stage.

3

———

"Holy shit!" the girl next to me sighed when she finally came down from her intense climax. "That was *insane*. I've never seen anything like that before, and I've been to a lot of these performances. Whatever that thing was that was gyrating in her pussy, I want one of those."

"I know what you mean," I said. "I've got a pretty extensive collection of sex toys at home, but I've never seen anything like that before. Watching her use it hands-free with her legs spread apart was incredibly erotic."

As the brightly illuminated bed and the sexy blonde girl receded into the shadows, the MC walked back onto the stage.

"Did you enjoy that performance?" she asked.

"Woo-hoo!" the audience roared in unison.

"Hold up a sec," the MC said, removing her decibel-monitoring app from of her pocket and tapping the screen.

"Now tell me what you *really* think!" she said, turning the device toward the crowd.

Everybody hollered at the top of their lungs, clapping enthusiastically. The needle swung ninety percent of the way around the arc before stopping near the end of the red zone.

"That's going to be pretty hard to beat," the girl sitting next to me smiled.

She turned and extended her hand over the armrest between us.

"My name's Ashley. I suppose we should introduce ourselves now that we've gotten to know each other a little better."

"Jade," I said, clasping her hand with my wet fingers. "Sorry about the mess–I guess I got a little carried away by that last performance."

"That makes two of us," Ashley said, removing some napkins from her gift bag and handing me a few tissues. "I think you need these more than I do," she said, wiping my juice off the front of her face. "I've never seen a girl squirt as much as you do. You should consider putting on a performance of your own. With your special powers, you'd have a shot at going all the way."

I nodded my head as I cleaned the back of the chair in front of me.

"It's crossed my mind a couple of times. I could sure use a free trip to the tropics. But I'm not sure I've got the nerve to take off all my clothes in front of a group of strangers. I'm enjoying things plenty enough from right here in the viewing gallery."

I watched Ashley remove the dripping dildo from her pussy and wipe it off with a napkin. "What about you? You put on a pretty erotic show yourself. With your hot body, I'm sure you'd get some very appreciative scores of your own."

"I've thought about it," she said. "I guess I just haven't found a strong enough reason to give it a try yet. I'm still thinking of ideas for what I could do that would be new and different."

After the stagehands finished remaking the bed, the MC returned to the stage to introduce the next act.

"That last performance received one of the highest scores in a long time," she said. "But if anyone can top her, I'm guessing this next act has one of the best shots. Prepare yourselves for *Sappho and Aphrodite!*"

The curtain at the side of the stage parted and two naked redheads emerged, walking hand-in-hand toward the bed in the center of the stage. They looked remarkably alike, with similar builds, height, and the same auburn ringlets falling gently over their shoulders. I wondered if they might be twins, and I turned toward Ashley, pinching my eyebrows in surprise.

"I didn't know they allowed tandem acts," I said.

"It happens every now and then," she nodded. "But most people prefer to go solo. It's hard to judge a tandem act in terms of who should move forward to the next round. Sometimes, the MC asks the crowd to rate each performer separately, but in this case these girls almost look like *clones* of one another. It would be impossible to differentiate the two when it comes time to evaluate their performance."

"Do you think they're *sisters*?" I said.

"I dunno, but if they are, that's just notched it up a couple of levels in my books. Let's see how far they take it."

As I ogled the figures of the two girls walking across the stage, my pussy twitched imagining them touching one another. Their skin shone like alabaster under the bright light of the overhead spotlight, their pink nipples glowing like beacons on the pale canvas of their bodies. Their tits were very small, making them almost look like adolescent boys with their flat chests and narrow hips. But when they reached the side of the bed and climbed onto the mattress, their curvy asses and sexy slits left little doubt as to their real sex.

"Mmm," Ashley purred, placing her feet on the armrests in front of her, spreading her thighs apart. "There's nothing like fresh girl meat to get me in the mood. *Two* helpings are making me twice as hungry."

My own pussy pulsed imagining them growing up together, playing in the privacy of their own rooms. Whether they were real sisters or it was just part of their act, I'd already bought into the theme as my juices began to trickle down under my ass.

"They're fucking hot, that's for sure," I nodded, hiking my skirt up to reveal my glistening mound.

"Damn girl," Ashley grunted. "You look pretty edible yourself. I might need to take you home once the show is over to have you for dessert."

"That can be arranged," I purred, giving her a playful wink.

When we turned our attention back to the stage, the girls were lying down beside each other, rubbing their bodies together as they kissed passionately on the bed.

"Something tells me this isn't the *first* time they've been together this way," Ashley mused.

"No," I nodded, my eyes glued on the stage. "I have a feeling they've had quite a few years to prepare for this moment."

As they intertwined their legs and began to grind their mounds together, Ashley and I began to circle our tingling clits with our right hands.

"Mmm," I moaned. "I'd love to feel their sweet bodies pressed up against mine right about now."

"Do you need a little *assist*?" Ashley said, raising an eyebrow and reaching over the armrest to slip her fingers under my blouse.

"*Fuck*, yes," I hissed, dying to feel someone else's hands on my body.

I spread my legs far apart and rested the underside of my knees over the adjacent armrests like the couple I'd seen at the previous show. Ashley took one look at my pink nub poking its head out of its sheath and placed her other palm over my pussy, caressing my folds with the tips of her fingers.

"Yes, baby," I groaned. "Play with my clit while I watch these cute girls. I want to imagine I'm right there in the thick of the action."

"You like flat-chested girls, do you?" she purred, lifting her fingers to circle my burning jewel.

"Yes," I panted. "I reminds me of my adolescent years."

"Mmm," Ashley mewed. "The great taboo. It's off limits now that we're grown up, but I remember experimenting when I was younger too. I bet those two have been playing with each other for a long time."

"Yes," I groaned, beginning to lose myself in the fantasy.

The two redheads suddenly separated and shifted into a scissor position, lying on their sides as they reached out and clasped hands.

"*Fuck me*," I groaned, watching the two girls rubbing their pussies together.

"Does that turn you on?" Ashley purred, slipping her fingers inside me as she trilled my clit with her thumb.

"You have *no* idea," I purred.

"Oh, I've got a pretty good idea judging by how wet you are," she said. "Are you going to squirt all over their pretty little tits?"

"Fuck yes," I groaned, getting more and more worked up watching the two girls tribbing their wet pussies together.

"What exactly would you do with them if you had the opportunity?" Ashley asked. "What did you use to do with your girlfriends during sleepovers?"

"I'd touch them in their private areas," I panted. "Kiss them, suck them, *probe* them."

Ashley peered at me with a sly smile.

"Trib them, mount them, grind your pussies together?"

"Yes," I groaned, reflecting back on my earliest sexual discoveries.

"Did you squirt back then too?" she asked.

"Not right away. Not until I went through puberty and began lubricating more heavily."

"Did you cum with your little friends?"

"Yes," I said, beginning to tremble from the imagery of the two girls scissoring on the stage, reminding me of my explorative youth.

"What else did you like to do with your pretty girlfriends?" Ashley said, using the show on the stage as a metaphor for reliving my childhood memories.

"Sometimes we'd play with toys..." I said.

As if on cue, one of the girls lifted a long green object from under the covers, placing it between their pussies.

A cucumber! I murmured, remembering the moment when my girlfriends and I discovered how much fun it was to probe our pussies with whatever phallic-shaped objects we could find. As the girls separated their bodies, placing the ends of the cucumber against each of their openings, my juices began pouring over Ashley's hands.

"Do you want me to place my little toy inside you while you channel fucking these girls?" Ashley said.

"Yes, please," I begged, desperate to feel my pussy filled up while I imagined fucking the cute redheads.

Ashley reached over and lifted her rabbit vibrator off her seat cushion and without even bothering to turn it on, she rammed it inside my pussy, beginning to fuck me with the dildo as she leaned over to kiss me. I turned my face toward her and moaned into her mouth as I peered at the spectacle on the stage out of the corner of my eyes. The two girls now had the double-sided dildo deeply embedded in each of their pussies as they ground their vulvas together, moaning in unison. I could see their arms beginning to tense up as they held each other tightly, while their passion slowly built toward a peak.

Ashley tapped the base of the rabbit dildo, activating the dual vibration functions, and I slid down in my seat, pressing the flapping rabbit ears against my pussy.

"Oh *God*, Ashley," I panted. "I'm going to cum baby. I'm going to cum so *hard*..."

As I watched the pre-orgasmic rash begin to spread over the chests of the two pale-skinned girls writhing together on the bed, my pleasure suddenly crested and I groaned a deep guttural growl. As the redheads began convulsing and wailing in union, the walls of my pussy clenched in powerful convulsions and I sprayed my juices out my plugged hole, ricocheting off the top of the vibrator towards Ashley's face.

While I thrashed in my seat squealing in ecstasy, she smiled at me, blinking her eyes between the sprays bouncing off her face while she held the vibrating dildo firmly against my vulva. Suddenly I became aware of similar noises in the theater as other viewers groaned in unison with the two girls shaking on the bed. The action of the two youthful-looking girls had brought back a flood of fond memories and it took a long time for me to stop coming as I watched them pleasure each other on the stage. When I finally came down from my high and collapsed back against my seat, Ashley looked over at me and smiled.

"We've *got* to get together soon," she mewed, lifting her dripping hand to my breast and pinching my erect nipple.

"Let's get out of here," I said, thrusting my tongue into her mouth. "I can't wait a moment longer."

"What about the rest of the show?" Ashley said, motioning to the MC walking back out onto the stage.

"*Fuck* the rest of the show," I said. "Let's make our *own* show. I need to feel your body next to mine before I go crazy."

Ashley paused for a moment, then peered at me with a sly grin. She raised herself out of her chair and sat her naked ass down over my still-fluttering pussy.

"Why wait any longer?" she said, tilting her pussy towards mine as she rested her arms on the seat rest in front of us. "Maybe we can have it *both* ways."

As she began to rock her hips against mine, I felt our clits merge as a new surge of energy rocketed through me. I grabbed her ass with both hands and pulled her closer toward me.

"Fuck yes," I purred. "Let's show these guys how it's really done..."

4

———————

After the show, Ashley and I went back to my place and made love all night long. Both of us had ideas for what we'd like to do for our own auditions, and we experimented with different positions and pairings for many hours. By the time I fell asleep at three a.m., I dreamed of all the adventurous things we might try on stage. In the morning, I slipped on a robe and went downstairs to cook up some breakfast and Ashley followed soon after.

"Mmm–that smells good," Ashley said, smelling the bacon and eggs frying in the pan.

"I thought you might be hungry after our little workout last night," I winked.

"*Little*?" she said, raising her eyebrows. "Between the two of us, we must have burned enough calories to light a small city."

I handed her a steaming mug of coffee and sat down on the bar stool next to her.

"That was pretty wild, wasn't it?"

"Are you referring to the action on the stage or how quickly we landed in each other's laps?"

"Both," I smiled. "I don't think I've come so hard as when you were grinding your pussy against mine while we watched the show together in the darkness."

"Viewing a live sex act can be pretty damn stimulating ," Ashley nodded. "I think it's genius what they've created there. I didn't realize how much I enjoyed being a voyeur until I discovered this production. But I think I'm just about ready to flip things around."

"Oh?" I said, lifting the food out of the skillet and placing it on her plate. "You think you're daring enough to bare everything in front of a group of strangers?"

"They won't *all* be strangers," she smiled, caressing my arm with the back of her hand. "*You'll* be there, right? It'll be that much more of a turn-on knowing you'll be watching too."

She paused for a moment as she wolfed down another spoonful of scrambled eggs.

"But it'll be even *more* exciting if we do it together."

"You mean as a tandem act, or each of us separately?"

"Both. It will be exciting for us to perform solo, but we can step it up to the next level if we decide to get together. That way, at least *one* of us will have a chance to win the trip to Mexico."

"You're just hedging your bets in case I win it for myself," I said, crunching on a piece of bacon.

"Well, if we each perform solo, we double our chances. Will you be my plus-one if I win?"

"Or you can be *mine* when *I* win," I smiled.

"Then when we get together as a couple, we can wow the crowd all over again," Ashley said. "It can only *help*, right?"

"I think you might be onto something," I nodded, finishing the last of my breakfast. "But now I've worked up a whole different kind of appetite. Do you feel like going back upstairs and working on some of our routines?"

"I thought you'd never ask," Ashley said, sliding her last piece of bacon sensuously between her lips.

❧

For the next couple of hours, Ashley and I bounced ideas back and forth as we play-acted our routines in front of one another, giving each other tips and encouragement for how we could ramp up the excitement level. Then we practiced every combination we could imagine for joining together while we watched ourselves in my dressing mirror. By the time we both fell asleep exhausted again, I felt I'd vastly improved my repertoire of girl-on-girl sex.

When the date for the next auditions rolled around, we tingled in excitement waiting in the wings for our turns to go on stage. The first performer was a pretty brunette dressed in a cowboy hat and pantless chaps. She carried a pommel-horse-shaped apparatus onto the stage, then placed it in the center of the bed and plugged it into the nearest power outlet. After screwing a diamond-shaped dildo into the middle of the saddle, she spent the next thirty minutes riding it like a bucking bronco, flailing her arms in the air as the plug vibrated inside her. By the time she'd finished riding it in the forward- and backward-cowgirl positions, Ashley and I estimated that she'd had least four orgasms.

The next performers were a tandem act, dressed in sexy super-hero costumes. The lower half of the Batgirl character's costume had been entirely cut away, with her naked ass and bare legs posing a sexy counterpoint to her well-camouflaged upper body covered with a black mask, tight rubber bodice, and flapping yellow cape. Her Catwoman sidekick had the front of her full-length bodysuit slit open down the front, pressing her large round breasts into a sexy cleavage exposed on the front of her chest. They'd had some additional props placed on the stage and the Catwoman character entered first, creeping furtively toward a nightstand at the side of the bed. She opened the drawer, peering nervously around her, then she tucked a jewelry box under her arm.

Suddenly, Batgirl entered from the other side of the stage and confronted the would-be burglar, placing her hands on her hips and shaking her head in disapproval. Catwoman pulled out a whip and snapped it toward her adversary, but the Batgirl used her quick reflexes to sidestep the rippling cord. Then she pulled a foam boomerang out of her utility belt and flung it at Catwoman, striking her in the head as she fell to the floor, pretending to be unconscious. She then carried the girl to the bed and tied her to the four bedposts using wrist ties from her utility belt, spreading her arms and legs in a wide V-shape.

It was only then that I noticed the crotch of Catwoman's tights had also been split open, revealing her pink vulva surrounded by the black bodysuit. As she woke up from her stupor and took stock of her predicament, she sneered at Batgirl, flailing her body helplessly against her binds. Batgirl simply smiled back at her and reached into her utility belt, pulling out a large penis-shaped vibrator. She flipped a button on the base and the dildo began buzzing and throbbing loudly. As Batgirl lowered it toward her captive's open crotch in a threatening gesture, Catwoman thrashed her body on the bed, pretending to be frightened.

The whole scene was over-the-top campy, but somehow the appearance of the two skimpily clad superheroes pretending to battle created a highly arousing effect. Ashley and I looked at one another shaking our heads in dismay, wondering the same thing.

"I didn't know we were allowed to wear *costumes* and use *props*," she said. "Do you think our act is going to be interesting enough after this performance?"

"Let's see what else they've got in their bag of tricks," I said. "Remember it's not about the size of your package, it's how well you can use it."

As we peered back out onto the stage, Batgirl placed the vibrating tip of the dildo against Catwoman's mound and she suddenly stopped flailing as she lifted her hips to press the device firmer against her vulva. Batgirl peered at her devilishly, then pulled the vibrator away from her pussy as Catwoman feigned frustration. Then she held it against her flapping thighs for a few more seconds before yanking it away once again. They continued this cat-and-mouse routine for a few minutes until Catwoman shook her body angrily, looking at Batgirl with pleading eyes.

Batgirl picked the jewelry case up off the floor and pointed toward it with a disapproving stare, then motioned toward the nightstand where it belonged. Catwoman nodded her head in acquiescence, then Batgirl placed the container back in the table and held the vibrator high up in the air for the audience to see. They cheered her loudly, encouraging her to place it back on Catwoman's twitching vulva. But this time she inserted the huge phallus into Catwoman's pussy until it was fully embedded inside her. Then she proceeded to pump it in and out of her hole as Catwoman became increasingly aroused, moaning and writhing on the mattress until she climaxed in a powerful orgasm. When they finished their routine, the audience roared in approval, clapping enthusiastically.

"That's gonna be pretty hard to beat," Ashley said, knowing it was her turn to go on next. "Maybe I should have dressed up in a costume or brought some extra props."

"Don't worry about what other people are doing," I assured her, squeezing her hand gently. "With your hot bod and your sexy routine, you'll have them eating out of your hands in no time."

"Or hopefully my *crotch*," she smiled at me nervously.

"Exactly," I said. "Go do your thing. Remember, I'll be here watching the whole time getting turned-on along with you."

"Mmm," Ashley purred. "That'll help. Maybe I won't need as much lube after all."

I smiled back at her, nudging her out the curtain, and she walked toward the newly remade bed with her hands resting in the side pockets of her robe. We'd both agreed that her act would be sexier if she revealed her body in stages, teasing the audience about what she intended to do on stage. When she reached the bed, she climbed up onto the mattress and straddled the brass headboard, placing one knee on the pillow and her other foot on the opposite rail for support.

She began rocking her hips sexily on the top rail and opened the front of her robe, showing her plump tits sitting high on her chest. As she slowly slid her body toward the corner bedpost, she peered up at me and I nodded, circling my hand over my crotch to signal how much her act was turning me on. When she reached the end of the rail, she grasped the small brass globe topping the post and rolled her hands over it like she was giving it a sexy hand job. But she and I both knew she was actually lubing the ball with some tissues she'd hidden in her pockets. Then she lifted herself up and straddled the post between her thighs, lowering herself down a few inches.

To the audience watching from an oblique angle, they couldn't have known immediately what she was doing, with her robe still covering half of her body. But for me watching directly in front of her, I could see that she'd embedded the brass finial deep inside her pussy. When she reached back and pulled her robe off her body, an audible gasp rose from the audience when they finally realized what she was doing. With appreciate applause wafting up from the seats, Ashley placed both of her hands on the top rail and began to rock her body up and down over the brass bulb. As it became obvious she was fucking the bedpost, many observers began to moan while they stimulated themselves watching her erotic act.

When she peered back over towards me, I was squeezing my right breast tightly while my other hand fluttered between my legs. I nodded at her quietly as my body began to tremble in concert with hers, losing myself in her performance. Even though we'd talked about what we planned to do once we were on stage, I hadn't realized how sexy it would be to watch her first hand with the audience buzzing around us.

As Ashley became increasingly aroused listening to the reaction of the audience, she turned her body to face them directly, spreading her knees wide apart so they could clearly see her impaled over the bedpost. Her movements began to pick up in intensity and her neck muscles started to tighten as she approached climax. Suddenly she lurched forward, jerking her body forward and back from the convulsions racking her body.

As I watched her shaking in the throes of agony, I came unconsciously watching my new friend pleasure herself in front of the large audience. After many long seconds of quivering in pleasure, she slowly lifted herself off the glistening pole and pulled her robe back over her body, scampering off the stage in my direction. As the lights fell over the platform, the audience cheered loudly in appreciation of her sexy and original performance.

5

———————

"What did you think?" Ashley said, scurrying up next to me.

"That was fucking hot," I said, holding her tightly as I motioned toward the still-buzzing amphitheater. "And judging by the audience reaction, *they* enjoyed it too. How did it feel being on stage? Were you nervous at all?"

"A little at first," she nodded. "But once I got that ball inside me, I wasn't thinking of much else. Other than watching *you,* of course. Knowing you were getting turned on watching me was more exciting than knowing everybody else was watching me."

"I'm glad," I said. "Did you enjoy yourself?"

"You have no idea," she smiled. "Let's just say the turnaround crew might need a little longer to clean up the bed in preparation for the next act.

"Speaking of which," she said, slipping her hand inside my robe to cup my quivering breast. "Are you ready to go out there? You seem a bit nervous yourself."

"That's just me still feeling excited from watching you. I've never felt more ready to do something like this in my whole life."

"Break a leg, babe," Ashley smiled. "Just make sure you don't break anything *else*." She held up her hands as I turned around for her to help me disrobe. "Are you sure you want to go out there completely naked?"

"It'll just get in the way," I said. "I just want it to be my naked body they're focused on. Hopefully that'll be enough."

"You don't need any props or extra embellishments," Ashley said. "You'll be doing something nobody's ever seen before."

"Wish me luck then," I said, hearing the MC come back out onto the stage to introduce the next act.

"You won't need it," Ashley said. "I'll see you soon."

I smiled back at her, knowing it would be sooner than anybody expected.

As the MC motioned toward the stagehands, the curtain swung open and I strutted across the stage, relishing every step as the audience took in my taut, hourglass figure. I'd worked hard to keep my thirty-something body in good shape and as I extended my legs with each step, wiggling my ass and holding my chest high, my body surged with fire. I was about to do something I'd never tried before, and the idea of touching myself in front of a room full of strangers electrified me.

When I reached the bed, I lay down on it face up and reached behind me to grasp the headrail with both hands. I could still feel traces of Ashley's lubrication on the bar, and it excited me as I pulled my legs up and over my head, showing the crowd my bald pussy and ass. A few girls hollered their approval, and I spread my legs into a wide 'V' so they could see my glistening bald pussy more easily. A few people applauded my limber body, but after the previous week's sexy contortionist act, I knew they were looking for something more.

I caressed the insides of my thighs, stopping tantalizingly short of my pink folds, then turned around and placed my hips against the headboard, tilting my head as I peered at the audience upside down. They cheered loudly at my taunting gesture, knowing it was just a warm-up for the main act. Then I lifted my legs straight up above my body and slowly lowered them backwards toward my head. I'd been working on my flexibility in the weeks leading up to the performance and didn't have any difficulty resting my toes on the surface of the bed a few feet behind my head.

At this point all the audience could see was the slit of my ass with my face concealed by my closed legs. As they continued to cheer me on, I began to spread my feet apart until my legs were separated about sixty degrees. I could have easily spread them further apart, but that wasn't the main purpose of my routine. I placed the palms of my hands over each of my buttock cheeks and pulled my hips further down, moving my dripping pussy closer to my face.

With my toes inching further down toward the foot of the bed, the audience slowly began to realize what I was trying to do. As a loud murmur spread across the auditorium, I watched my slit move ever-closer to my puckering lips. With my erect clit quivering only inches from my mouth, I tilted my head back and peered toward the audience again, licking my lips in anticipation.

Realizing I was only inches away from taking my glistening gland into my mouth, their cheers grew in increasingly loud as I pressed my feet further down the mattress, lowering my box closer to my waiting mouth. Even though I'd practiced this hundreds of times before, knowing that so many eyes were watching me from the darkened auditorium raised my excitement to a whole new level. As my juices poured out of my slit over the top of my mound, I pulled my hips forward with one last tug, enveloping my hot gland with my moist lips.

A loud gasp suddenly arose from the audience, who'd never expected me to accomplish this feat of gymnastic elasticity. As I began to circle my tongue around my bright red jewel, a series of loud moans emanated from every corner of the auditorium. The crowd's reaction to my unique form of self-stimulation only increased my excitement as I lowered my hips even further, stroking my glistening slit up and down with my outstretched tongue. It was obvious that no one in the audience had ever seen anyone do anything remotely like this before, and I smiled as I listened to their shocked reaction.

As I licked the sides of my labia, pausing for long moments to suck my erect clit, I spread my legs further apart so they could see my pink pucker shining between my ass cheeks. I was putting every part of me out there for display, and the eroticism of the act lifted my passion with every passing moment. As I began to feel my pleasure rising toward its inevitable peak, I turned my face toward Ashley watching from the wings, and I nodded my head gently.

We'd both choreographed this routine carefully, and it was *her* I really wanted to cum with, not just the audience. Ashley dropped her robe on the floor and began walking onto the stage in my direction. When the audience saw that I'd enlisted an accomplice into my sexy act, their cheer rose even louder.

When Ashley reached the edge of my bed, she positioned herself behind my hips, peering down into my splayed, glistening slit. She smiled sexily at me, then grabbed one of her tits and leaned forward, stroking it against my wet opening. As she slid it toward my quivering mound, I popped my clit out of my mouth and began sucking on her nipple, alternating between her erect nub and mine. As the groans from the appreciative audience grew louder and louder, we smiled at each other, knowing we'd created something new and memorable.

But we were far from finished titillating the crowd, and I was still aching to come. I'd been holding back my orgasm until she joined me on the bed and as she peered into my glassy eyes, she pulled her body back until her face nestled directly between my thighs. While I resumed sucking my burning glans, she slowly licked my slit downward until she reached my pink rosebud. Without pausing for a second, she began circling my pucker with her long outstretched tongue, as my face began to turn redder and redder in mounting ecstasy.

As I felt my orgasm begin to wash over me, we locked eyes and I grunted loudly as my pussy began to clench in powerful contractions. I squirted my pent-up juices out of my pussy all over Ashley's pretty face embedded between my quivering cheeks. With my lips locked over my twitching clit and my entire body convulsing on the bed, I watched the muscles on the underside of my vulva pulsing as I sprayed squirt after squirt over Ashley's face mere inches in front of me.

The theater was now awash in the sounds of simultaneous orgasms as girls jilled themselves excitedly watching the two of us joined together in one of the sexiest routines they'd ever witnessed. Ashley reached between her legs and moaned into my crevasse as she popped off with the rest of the crowd. By the time I'd finished spraying her face and my clit stopped pulsing in my mouth, she leaned forward and kissed me passionately between my legs. As we lay there together for a long moment reveling in the reaction of the crowd, we nodded toward each other knowing we'd created a once-in-a-lifetime performance.

But we still had one ace up our sleeves to guarantee that at least one of us would be moving forward in the competition. With a sly grin, Ashley raised herself off the bed and straddled her feet between my hips as she peered down at my dripping crotch. Then she slowly squatted her body down until her ass cheeks rested against mine. I pulled my legs forward a few inches and bent my knees, tilting my hips backwards her until our pussies touched.

As we began to rock our bodies together, I watched her labia twisting and stretching against mine while we moaned in delirious pleasure. I was already buzzing from my last orgasm, and as we angled our hips toward one another, our clits touched and we gasped when we felt our sensitive organs melding together. As her slippery ass slid effortlessly over mine from our combined juices still coating our bodies, she reached down to hold my hands. I intertwined my fingers with hers as I peered into her eyes, feeling another powerful orgasm beginning to overtake me.

The feeling of her erect clit rolling over mine as our asses rubbed together was sublime. Although we'd experimented with the routine in the days leading up to this week's performance, there was something about the audacity of performing it live in front of a crowd of strangers that raised the excitement level even higher for both of us. As Ashley's mouth began to spread open while she approached another powerful orgasm, she peered down at me and mouthed the words *I love you*. By now, neither of us were paying any attention to the moans and groans emanating from the audience as we gripped each other's hands tightly while our pleasure consumed us.

Suddenly, Ashley let out a howl as her body began convulsing overtop of my hips. Watching her come with her pussy joined together with mine quickly put me over the edge also as I began spraying out in every direction from the tight seal between us. While I watched the spectacle from my prone position with my juices splashing all over our tits and faces, I saw my rosebud clamping rhythmically inches from my face. When we both finally finished shaking in a uniform mash of merged flesh, Ashley dropped down onto the bed beside me and kissed me gently.

"If *that* doesn't get us a free trip to the Desire resort in Mexico," she panted, "I don't know what will."

I peered over toward her and smiled.

"Who needs a trip to Mexico when we've got all the stimulation we need right here?"

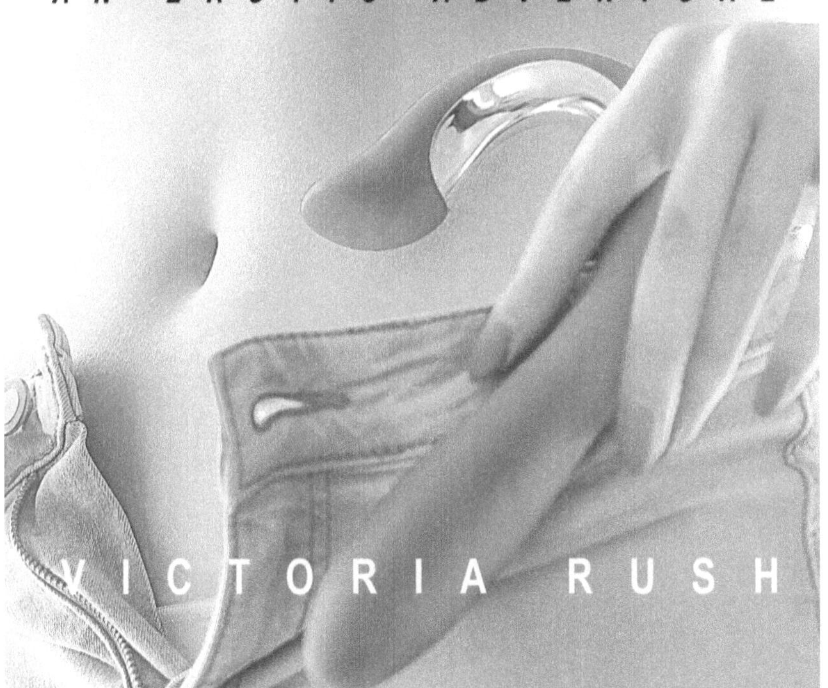

THE
DARE

AN EROTIC ADVENTURE

VICTORIA RUSH

1

———————

"Do you have any more cases that need my help?" I asked my best friend and certified sex therapist, Hannah, at our weekly get-together lunch.

Ever since the last time she'd invited me to sit in on one of her sessions, I'd fantasized about watching another one of her clients release her inhibitions while learning how to orgasm for the first time.

"I'm afraid Haley was a one-off," Hannah said. "That was definitely pushing the envelope in terms of how far I can take the concept of a guided session."

"But you said many of your clients are open to the idea of using a surrogate to help them overcome their fear of intimacy?"

"Yes, but bringing a third party into the equation is stretching the limits of client confidentiality."

"Not if they agree to it up front and sign a consent form."

"True. But I'm already drifting into unchartered territory using this unconventional form of sex therapy. I'm supposed to just *talk* to them, not watch them while they touch themselves."

I shook my head as I sliced into my grilled salmon.

"You just want to have them all to *yourself*," I winked.

"Maybe," Hannah smiled, noisily sipping her margarita. "But my hands-on approach seems to be working."

"How's Haley doing these days, anyway?" I said, wondering about the pretty co-ed I'd shared an intimate encounter with. "Is she still receiving treatment?"

"The last I heard, she was in a committed relationship with another girl at college. She said her sex life was very satisfying. Apparently, that blended session with you helped her turn the corner."

"Glad I could help," I said, crossing my knees under the table to quiet my tingling clit as I remembered watching Haley come between my legs. "Happy to hear we cured another dysfunctional patient."

"You shouldn't be so dismissive of other women's problems," Hannah said, looking at me disapprovingly. "The inability to orgasm is far more prevalent than people think, especially among women. It's often caused by a traumatic episode in their past or severe childhood repression. Not everyone's as lucky as you and me to have had a healthy upbringing."

"I'm sorry," I said. "You're right. I remember how unsatisfying my first marriage was. We were both raised in a conservative household that frowned upon any form of sexual expression before marriage. All Jason seemed interested in was doing the missionary position in the dark. I hardly even had a chance to get aroused before he popped off. It wasn't until I discovered sex with other *women* that I really learned to enjoy myself."

"You're lucky that you found a successful outlet for your desires at a relatively young age," Hannah nodded. "You've come a long way since then."

"Literally and figuratively," I chuckled. "I can hardly believe how enjoyable my sex life has become. My orgasms are stronger and more powerful than I ever imagined. And the best part is how *long* I can make it last. It's almost like I can turn it on and off at will, holding out until the best optimal moment."

"You mean coming simultaneously with your partner?"

"Most of the time, yes. But sometimes I like to wait until *she's* finished coming so I can concentrate on maximizing her pleasure."

"Maybe you should become a partner in my therapy practice," Hannah said, lifting an eyebrow. "It sounds like you've mastered your art. I could use another colleague to juggle my growing caseload."

"Ha!" I chuckled. "I'm afraid I could never have your discipline. I'd want to jump the clients every time instead of just talking them through their process of self-discovery. You'd lose your license in no time if you brought me on as a full partner."

Hannah paused for a moment as she took another sip of her cocktail.

"Maybe we should *test* the premise and see just how disciplined you really are. You say you can turn your desire on and off at will. I bet you wouldn't be able to control yourself so easily under the right circumstances."

"How do you mean?" I said, suddenly intrigued. "Under what circumstances?"

Hannah peered at me with a devilish grin.

"I think if we put you in a highly charged sexual situation and took away your ability to control the level of stimulation you received, that I could make you pop off whenever I wanted."

"Like *what*?" I said, leaning forward on the table. "What did you have in mind?"

"I've actually been thinking about this for a while," Hannah smiled. "Ever since we were at this same restaurant and you tried out my new sex toy under the table. It gave me some fresh ideas for how we could take it to the next level."

"That was pretty fucking hot," I nodded, feeling my panties begin to dampen at the thought of Hannah watching me squirm in my seat while I was surrounded by restaurant patrons quietly eating their meals. "How could you possibly make that any more arousing?"

"You have *no* idea," Hannah smirked, lifting her glass back up to her lips.

2

"You can't leave me hanging like that!" I huffed, slamming my fists down on the table. "What kind of evil plan are you cooking up?"

Hannah peered at me as she took another bite of her shrimp salad. She was enjoying torturing me while my mind raced trying to imagine what she was concocting. When she swallowed her mouthful and washed it down with another sip of wine, I looked at her pleadingly, holding up my hands up in despair.

"What if we made your next sexual encounter a *one-way* affair, instead of a partnered experience?" she said.

"I've already tried every type of self-stimulation, using every toy imaginable. I think I've mastered the art of orgasm control via masturbation many times."

"Not when somebody *else* is controlling the toy."

My eyes suddenly flew open as I began to realize what Hannah had in mind.

"You mean using some kind of remote-control device?" I said. "I've heard about those and always wanted to give it a try."

"But not in a public place," Hannah smiled.

"*What!*" I said, jerking back in my chair. "Why would you want to do that? Wouldn't you already have all the power you need control-ling the level of stimulation I receive watching me one-on-one?"

"That would be too simple," she said. "Kind of like a staring contest. In the absence of any distractions, it would just be mind over matter. But in a public setting it won't be so easy for you to stay focused. Plus, the consequences will be more serious if you do lose control."

I leaned forward and calmly ate another bite of my salmon, pretending to be unfazed.

"In the unlikely event that you could actually force me to reach orgasm on your terms, I'd just bite my lip and cross my legs, and no one would be any the wiser."

Hannah speared another piece of shrimp and raised it to her mouth, sucking on it teasingly.

"You're forgetting about that *other* feature of your sexual powers, which is your tendency to squirt when you come. If I can make you come in a public place, it will be almost impossible for everyone to not know what's happening."

I placed my hands on the edge of the table and pushed my chair backwards, scrunching my face in dismay.

"You are truly evil," I said. "What kind of sick person would dream up such a crazy scenario?"

"Your best friend and lover, for one," Hannah smiled.

"*You're on!*" I said, slamming my cocktail down on the table. "But what's in it for me if I win? Do I get a silent stake in your practice?"

"I think it's best we continue your role as a special consultant. I think we can use you more effectively as a mutual participant when the need arises. I was thinking of something we can *both* enjoy."

"Such as?"

"We've both talked about you much we'd love to go to Bora Bora. If I can make you lose control in public, you'll have to pay for the airfare. But if you're as good as you say you are, then *I'll* pay for the flights. What do you say–are you up for the challenge?"

"Possibly," I said, getting wetter by the moment imagining Hannah's crazy idea. "But exactly what kind of public settings are we talking about? It's only fair that you let me know what I'm getting myself into before I take the leap."

"No dice," Hannah said, crossing her arms. "If you're as skilled as you're making yourself out to be, it shouldn't matter what the setting is. Half the fun will be in your not knowing until we get there."

I paused for a long moment, running my eyes over Hannah's face, trying to divine her thoughts.

"Fine," I said, holding out my hand across the table. "But this'll be quite a switch for you—encouraging a client *not* to reach orgasm for a change."

"Quite the contrary," Hannah smiled, clasping my hand. "It's fully aligned with the vision of my practice. I've never yet had a client who failed to achieve sexual fulfillment. But as I always like to tell them—most of the fun is in the process of *getting* there."

3

———————

"Okay, so now that I'm committed, tell me where you had in mind for this little experiment."

"Actually," Hannah said, "I have a *series* of places in mind, each one more challenging than the one before."

"But I thought you said this was a one-off proposition?"

"I said nothing of the sort. I only said that if you won, I'd pay for the flights to Bora Bora. If you want me to cover the cost of hotels, food, and all the other incidentals, you'll have to pass progressively tougher tests. We don't want to make this *too* easy for you, do we?"

I crossed my arms and huffed, putting on my best pouty face.

"It hardly seems fair," I said. "But I'm still game. Besides, either one of us can pull out at any time to lock in our gains, right?"

"I suppose so," Hannah shrugged. "But what would be the fun in that? Something tells me once you've tried the first experiment, you won't want to stop. I think you're going to find this whole thing quite titillating and exciting. This will be the most fun either one of us has had in a long time."

I pushed the rest of my half-eaten salmon dish to the side, suddenly no longer interested in eating.

"Okay, lay it on me then. Where are you planning to take me for the first test?

Hannah gulped down the rest of her margarita then peered at me with a lopsided grin.

"Church. More specifically, a *Catholic* church. You haven't been in quite a while, have you? This will be your chance to repent and atone for all your sins."

"It's not like I've broken any commandments or anything–"

"The Catholic Church still considers sex outside of marriage a mortal sin. So technically, you've been doing a ton of sinning since your marriage ended."

"Well I haven't been a practicing Catholic for ages," I snorted. "So my conscience is clear. This'll be a cakewalk. All I have to do is sit quietly in my pew, right?"

"Yes, but it'll be a *front-row* pew, in full view of the priest who'll be delivering the sermon."

"Okay, but I'll be fully clothed, right? It's not like there'll be anything for him to see..."

"Not if you can keep your composure and don't cum all over the floor," Hannah said, cocking her head playfully.

"I don't think I'll have any difficulty keeping my dick in my pants, in a manner of speaking. But you raise a good point. You can't expect me not to get a little wet while you're stimulating me. What will I be allowed to wear?"

"I assume you'll dress appropriately, wearing your Sunday best. A mid-length skirt and button-up blouse should do the trick. You should be able to hide a few dribbles that way, right?"

"I suppose so, but how will we muffle the sound of the vibrator buzzing inside my panties? There's likely to be other people sitting around me in adjacent pews..."

"Never fear," Hannah smiled, reaching into her purse and pulling out a U-shaped silicone sex toy. "I've been talking with our friend at the local Babeland store. She's given me the latest prototype of the We-Vibe vibrator to test." She held up a smaller device with two control buttons and a flywheel. "Complete with a Bluetooth remote control. And the best thing is that it's whisper-quiet.

"Here," she said, handing me the flexible device. "See for yourself."

She tapped one of the buttons on the remote and the thick side of the contraption began buzzing softly in my hand.

"Okay," I nodded, looking around me to see if any other restaurant patrons were distracted by the gentle hum of the object. "It's *quiet* enough, but which end goes inside?"

"The bulbous end is a natural G-spot stimulator. You place the flatter end against your clit, then pull the thing up tight against your vulva to keep it snugly in place."

I suddenly became mindful of the wetness permeating my panties as I imagined the device vibrating inside me, surrounded by a bunch of oblivious bystanders.

"Can I give it a try here, like we did last time?" I grinned.

"No way," Hannah said, pulling the toy out of my hands. "There'll be no trial runs for this or any future tests. You'll just have to wait until we get to the church."

"And where will *you* be sitting while this is all going down?" I said.

"Right next to you, of course. I'll want a front-row seat to watch all the action."

On Sunday morning, Hannah picked me up and drove me the two miles to our local church. The entire time I squirmed in my seat trying to imagine what it would be like having a vibrator buzzing inside me in the quiet chapel. When we got to the church parking lot, she pulled into a sheltered space then plucked the blue vibrator out of her purse and handed it to me, resting her arm on the seat cushion expectantly.

"*What?*" I said. "You don't trust me to put it in privately?"

"Not really," she smirked. "For all I know, you might pull on some adult diapers under your skirt to hide any unintended releases. Here," she said, handing me a plastic vial. "I brought some lube to make it go in easier."

"I don't need any," I said, pulling the vibrator out of her hands and placing it under my skirt. "I'm already plenty worked up thinking about this scenario."

"I hope you're wearing panties under that skirt," Hannah said, watching me shift my weight as I placed the device against my vulva. "We wouldn't want it popping out at an inopportune moment."

"I'll just have to leave that up to your imagination," I sneered, lifting my skirt halfway up my thigh. "Unless you need to inspect the goods to make sure I'm not cheating."

"I trust you," Hannah smiled, opening her car door. "Something tells me you're looking forward to this just as much as I am."

As we approached the entrance to the church, I noticed a familiar figure standing at the top of the steps greeting the incoming parishioners, and he made eye contact with me when Hannah and I approached the landing.

"Jade!" Father Fife said, holding out his hands to me. "I haven't seen you in such a long time. It's so good to have you join us again."

"I'm sorry, Father," I said, placing my sweaty hand between his. "I've been a little distracted lately..."

"Life has a habit of getting in the way of the important things," he said. "We're just glad to have you whenever you can find time." He turned to Hannah, raising his eyebrows in curiosity. "And who's this lovely lady you've brought with you to attend our service today?"

"This is Hannah," I said, motioning toward my friend. "I thought I'd bring her along for moral support."

"Happy to have you, Hannah," Father Fife said, clasping Hannah's hands warmly. "The Lord knows we all need moral support wherever we can find it."

Hannah nodded politely, then the two of us walked through the entrance doors where I dipped my hand into the bowl of holy water and crossed my chest before continuing on toward the front of the chapel.

"*Jesus*," Hannah whispered, peering around the imposing shrine.

"Is it just me, or did that feel a little creepy? All that talk about *having* us and that prolonged hand-holding. Hasn't he been paying any attention to the me-too movement?"

"I'm not sure any of that applies to men of the *cloth*," I chuckled. "But you better be careful about using the Lord's name like that around here. If anybody overhears you, you're liable to be burned at the stake."

The two of us stepped lively down the main aisle and finding a free spot in the front row, we took our seats flanked by two elderly couples. It was hard to imagine how Hannah would be able to use the remote-control device sandwiched so closely between other parishioners, and I crossed my legs, thankful for the brief respite. When everyone had filed into the chapel and the bell signaled the start of the service, a hush fell over the chamber and we all stood up as Father Fife walked onto the pulpit in his flowing robes.

"In the name of the Father, and of the Son, and of the Holy Spirit," he intoned solemnly.

"Amen," the congregation murmured in unison.

"The Lord be with you," he said.

"And with your spirit," the couples beside me retorted.

What the hell have I gotten myself into? I thought, feeling the flexible vibrator pressing against the inside of my closed legs. I didn't consider myself a terribly religious person, but being in this holy place surrounded by all the familiar rituals brought back all the old memories from my parents about the consequences of sinful behavior. *Surely getting secretly stimulated by a sex toy in the house of God will send me straight to hell.*

This was the point in the church service where everybody was supposed to take a moment to make a penitential act. While I listened to the other parishioners around me making their supplications, my knees began shaking as I made my own silent prayer for forgiveness.

"May Almighty God have mercy on us all," the priest said. "Forgive us our sins, and bring us to everlasting life."

"Amen," I joined in the congregation's response.

"Let us pray," Father Fife said, bowing his head.

As we closed our eyes and he began his opening prayer, Hannah nudged me with her knee and my mind raced with images of the pastor scornfully looking down at us while we played our blasphemous game. I peered up as he flapped his Bible closed, and caught him glancing in my direction.

"Through our Lord Jesus Christ, your Son," he said. "Who lives and reigns with you in the unity of the Holy Spirit, one God forever and ever."

"Amen," I said aloud, hoping he'd see me behaving like a good Catholic girl and turn his attention elsewhere.

He motioned for everyone to sit down and I was glad to get off my shaky feet onto the relative safety of the wooden pew.

"Good morning, ladies and gentlemen," he began his homily. "Today, I would like to talk with you about *morality*. Specifically, about the decaying state of society's morals in today's world. All around us we are surrounded by prurient symbols of modern decadence. First it was in the form of the printed word, then motion pictures, then the ubiquitous internet. It seems everywhere we turn, we are bombarded with profane and sacrilegious images."

I felt my heart pounding in my chest, like he was singling me out personally for my not-so-infrequent porn surfing.

"We seem to have forgotten," he railed, "the Lord's commandment that we shall not covet thy neighbor's wife. This admonition can be taken in its broadest context. Not only have many of you forsaken the sacred institution of marriage, but the egregious and widespread popularity of obscene *pornography* belies our unbridled lust and depravity. God slew Onan for spilling his seed, and so He will strike all others who practice self-abuse."

Hannah nudged her knee against mine, suddenly reminding me why we were here. I was glad that she hadn't yet had the opportunity to take out her remote-control device, and I prayed that we'd be able to get through most of the service without her rudely interrupting it. I'd already begun to regret agreeing to this little venture, and I hoped that somehow we'd be able to bypass this first phase in her experiment.

"I'd like you to pick up your Bibles," Father Fife said, interrupting my thoughts. "And turn to Mark, Chapter 7, Verse 20."

Hannah and I reached down to pick up the bibles lying on the seat beside each of us, and we flipped to the indicated section.

"Read this passage with me, my friends," Father Fife instructed. "What comes *out* of a person is what defiles him," he enunciated, while the congregation quietly murmured along.

As I began to recite the passage along with him, I saw Hannah reach into her side pocket and place her closed hand between the book binding.

"For from within come evil thoughts," I continued reading as I peered out of the corner of my eye to see what she was up to.

"Sexual immorality, adultery, coveting, wickedness..." we read in unison.

Suddenly, I felt the interior end of the vibrator begin to tremble inside me and I stuttered, trying to finish the passage.

"Deceit...sensuality...envy..." I stammered, trying to catch my breath as I followed along. Hearing my labored recital, Hannah turned her head in my direction, acknowledging my silent suffering. She knew exactly what I was feeling and how difficult it was for me to remain composed as I read the script.

"All these evil things...come from *within*," I gulped as I began to feel the pleasure spread across my pelvic region. "And they defile a person."

"Consider these words carefully," the priest said, surveying my hunched-over posture. "For the Lord does not abide salacious thoughts and behavior. If you want passage into His Kingdom, you must be as pure and righteous as He."

He paused for a moment to let the message sink in, then he motioned with his two hands for us to be seated. I was grateful for the rest, and I froze upright in my chair trying to ignore the movement of the possessed instrument inside me.

"Let us consider for a moment *another* one of God's ten commandments," Father Fife continued. "Thou shall not commit *adultery*. The Lord made Eve from the flesh of Adam, and in so doing signified that forever more man shall be united to his wife as one..."

As Father Fife ramped up the intensity of his gayphobic critique, so did Hannah, furtively adjusting the flywheel on the remote-control device nestled under her palm in her lap. As she slowly increased the speed of the vibrations emanating inside my pussy, I squirmed on the bench, trying to restrain my rising passion.

"By rejecting the sanctity of marriage," Father Fife continued, glancing distractedly in my direction, "you have all *sinned*. In the book of Deuteronomy, we saw that God ordered adulterers be stoned to death. For your indiscriminate behavior, so shall the Lord indiscriminately smite thee."

Jesus, I thought. If that's what awaits a sinner for cheating on their spouse, I wonder what happens to someone who self-abuses herself while sitting for Sunday Service in a house of God. *Surely I'll burn in hell for this act of sacrilege.*

Just when I thought I was beginning to get control over the delicious sensations stimulating my insides, Father Fife instructed us to stand once again and recite another passage from the Bible.

"Please stand now and read Peter 1:16 with me," he said.

Everyone stood and dutifully flipped to the relevant section of the scriptures. This time it was even harder for me to stand motionless, as my knees fluttered unsteadily from the pleasurable sensations radiating inside me.

"It is written..." I tried to read along. "That you shall be holy, for I am holy."

I saw Hannah's hands moving once again inside her prayer book, and suddenly I felt the *other* end of the U-shaped vibrator buzzing against my clit.

"And now Galatians 5:16," Father Fife instructed, barely giving me a chance to recover.

I flipped to the new citation and gasped for breath as my legs wobbled beneath me.

"But I say," I panted unsteadily. "Walk by the Spirit, and you will not gratify the desires of the flesh."

"So it is written," Father Fife said, closing his Bible. "Be righteous as the Lord, and you shall join him in Heaven for everlasting days. And now," he said, magnifying my torture. "I would like us to sing together one of my favorite hymns celebrating His blessing, *Amazing Grace*. Please pick up your hymn books and turn to page forty-three."

"Amazing grace, how sweet the sound," the priest began to sing as the entire congregation joined him in harmony.

"That saved a wretch like me," I sang along, trying to ignore the message that seemed targeted directly at me. As I tried to hold the melody, Hannah cupped the remote-control device in her hand and turned the flywheel to its maximum setting.

"I once was lost, but now am found," I hyperventilated, pressing my legs together as hard as I could to stifle the rising passion that threatened to overtake me.

"Was blind, but now I see," I squealed, singing the last word decidedly off-pitch as Father Fife turned to see my entire body shaking as I belted the famous hymn.

By the time I'd finished the song, I'd somehow managed to keep it together and fight off the cresting passion that had threatened to put me over the edge. When we finally sat back down, Hannah mercifully turned the vibrator off, and I spread my hands over my ruffled skirt to signal that I'd managed to keep myself composed.

When the service was over and we walked up the aisle behind the rest of the assembly to exit the church, I couldn't wait to get out of the building to wash myself off, figuratively and literally. I was glad that we were at the back of the crowd so nobody could see the back of my skirt. I wasn't sure if my leaking pussy had left a stain, but I sure as hell didn't want one of the parishioners pointing it out. When we finally exited the entrance doors, Father Fife turned to the two of us and smiled.

"I noticed you seemed a little more passionate than usual reciting today's passages, Jade" he said to me.

"Yes, Father," I said, shaking his hand unsteadily. "I felt truly embodied by the spirit."

"And *you*, Hannah," he nodded. "Did you enjoy today's service also?"

"Oh yes," she said. "It was the most moving sermon I've attended in a long time."

"I hope you'll both come again," Father Fife said to the two of us.

"I'm sure we *will*, Father," Hannah smiled as we continued down the steps.

Like the second we get back home, I thought to myself, dying to tear off my clothes and squirt all over Hannah's face while she ate out my still-dripping pussy.

4

———

"So what did you think?" Hannah said once we got in the car. "Did you find the experience uplifting?"

"I think you're *evil*," I said, reaching under my dress and pulling the vibrator out of my pussy. "You know we're both going to *hell* for that."

"At least we'll know how to enjoy ourselves once we get there," Hannah smirked.

"So, did I pass the test?" I said, inspecting the toy that had caused me so much torture minutes earlier.

"That was pretty impressive," Hannah nodded. "I particularly enjoyed watching you try to finish singing Amazing Grace."

"I practically burst a gasket during that one. Especially when Father Fife looked in my direction."

"That was fucking hilarious," Hannah laughed. "I loved his comment about how *moved* you seemed by the service. I still can't believe he didn't suspect any foul play."

"Maybe he *did*, but he was too embarrassed to admit it. Either way, I'll never be able to show my face again in this church after that little stunt. If *he* doesn't strike me down, then surely the Lord on high will."

"But it was worth it though, right?" Hannah said, angling out of the church parking lot. "It was insanely hot watching you shudder and squirm during the prayers and recitals. Didn't you find it incredibly exciting trying to control yourself in public?"

"How can you be so sure I *did*?" I said, flexing the U-shaped vibrator in my hands. "Maybe I experienced my own little rapture when you weren't looking."

"Oh *please*," Hannah said, stopping at the turnoff to my subdivision. "You don't think I *know* you by now after all the times we've made love? You were never good at hiding your orgasms. Besides your noisy vocalizations, you have a distinct way of contorting your body when you come. Not to mention the tidal wave you produce after a long buildup. Father Fife would have had to send in *Noah's Ark* to save all the believers once you opened the floodgates."

"Speaking of..." I said, placing my hand between her legs as she pulled into my driveway. "If you don't finish what you started, I'm going to spring a leak. Now be a good girl while I sit on your face."

Hannah and I rushed upstairs, where it only took a few seconds for me to pop off while she sucked my aching clit into her mouth. After we both came hard reliving the excitement of the church experience, we flopped back down onto the bed, giggling like two little girls.

"Thanks," I panted. "I needed that."

"That was pretty crazy, wasn't it?" she said. "I still can't believe we got away with it. Front row seat and all."

I rolled over onto my side and propped my head on my elbow as I peered into her eyes.

"It's pretty hard to imagine how you'll be able to step it up after that. What could possibly be harder than trying to hide having sex in a church?"

"Actually, if you think about it, that was almost too easy. After all, hardly anybody was looking at you the whole time. Everybody was focused on the priest or their prayer books. All you had to do was bite your lip and squeeze your legs together under your dress. At the *next* venue, people are going to have a harder time keeping their eyes off of you."

"Why?" I said, darting my eyes over her face trying to imagine what she was scheming. "Are you going to have me sing karaoke or put me in a wet t-shirt contest or something?"

"Not quite," she smiled. "But those aren't bad ideas. No, this next time you're going to be in a public library."

"That doesn't sound so difficult," I said, pulling back. "Everybody will be busy reading a book or searching the stacks."

"Oh, they'll be searching the *stacks* alright," she said, peering down at my plump breasts. "The way I'm going to have you dressed, not many people will be focused on *reading*. Plus, this time there won't be the sound of the preacher's voice or the congregation's singing to cover up your moans and groans. It'll be quiet as a mouse in there."

"Okay..." I said, trying to imagine myself in this new setting. "But where will you be this time?"

"I'll be at an adjacent table, providing a whole *different* kind of kind of distraction."

"No problem," I huffed. "I'll just close my eyes and think about dead cats or something."

"Uh-uh," Hannah said, shaking her head and blinking her eyes at me playfully. "You've got to be fully present in the moment if you want to prove you can control yourself. The whole point of these public displays is for you to show that you can turn it on and off as easily as you said you could."

"Fine," I said. "But you keep adding all these restrictions. What *other* ground rules do I need to know about?"

"You just need to look at me for the duration of the test. *All* of me—both what's going on above and below the table. And you have to remain upright in your seat the whole time. No slouching and trying to hide your best assets."

"You're such a *tease!*" I said, leaning in to bite her nipples. "How long do I have to do this? You can't possibly torture me any longer than the hour you just put me through at the church service."

Hannah cradled my head and wiggled her body down until we made eye contact again.

"Since we'll be ramping up the *other* sources of distraction, I suppose it's only fair that we cut down on the length of this test. Do you think you can survive a half hour without coming?"

"*Pshaw!*" I snorted. "After the church experience, this'll be a cake-walk. When were you thinking of doing this?"

Hannah paused for a moment to consider her options.

"The libraries are busiest on the weekends, but we don't want too many distractions stealing attention away from your performance. How about Wednesday afternoon around three in the afternoon? There should be just enough mid-day traffic around that time to keep everybody amused."

"You're on!" I said, rolling on top of her, pressing my mound against her pussy. "But you don't mind if I try to build up my immunity before then, do you? I figure the more cums I can get in ahead of time, the easier it will be to stem the floodwaters."

"By all means," she said, spreading her legs and tilting her hips until our clits touched. "I want to enjoy living out the fantasy as much as *you* do."

On the day of the library visit, Hannah came over to my place an hour early to supervise my preparation. She wanted to make sure I was dressed provocatively enough to attract the attention of the library visitors, both male and female. After trying on a variety of outfits, she finally settled on a tight-fitting tube-top and miniskirt with no underwear. Although my naughty parts were covered up by the opaque fabric, my ample-sized tits and curvy hips left little to the imagination as to what was underneath. This time, I'd be letting it all hang out for everyone to see.

When we got to the library, Hannah found an open table for me to sit in the main atrium, then she positioned herself at an adjacent table about ten feet away. I found a thick textbook resting on the counter and I pulled it over in front of me, hoping to block the view of my pointy tits protruding out of my stretchy tube top. At first, the library was thinly populated, and I shook my head impatiently, wondering what was keeping her from getting started. I was eager to complete the test before it got too busy, but she simply smiled back at me, spreading her legs slowly to reveal her bald pussy. She'd obviously scoped out the place ahead of time, and I scowled at her for making my task even more difficult.

Within ten minutes or so, the library began to fill up as students and office workers began to flit in after class and work hours. A pretty co-ed took a seat kitty-corner to me at my table, while a young stud in an expensive suit plopped some law books down on the table next to Hannah. Whether he was more interested in securing a position to see *me* better or to be next to Hannah, was unclear. Either way, both of them would have prime viewing access to me from their positions.

After tapping out a few messages on their phones, the two visitors opened their books and lowered their heads to begin reading. Within seconds, I felt the familiar tremble of the vibrator fluttering inside me, and I jumped in surprise. The pretty co-ed peered up at me with pinched eyebrows and I turned the page in my encyclopedia, pretending to be absorbed in my reading material. Suddenly, I felt the buzzing sensation of the *internal* branch of the vibrator turn to maximum and I jerked my head up to stare at Hannah in protest. She shook her head disapprovingly, while motioning with her two fingers to keep my gaze focused on her.

I nodded in capitulation, and she dimmed the vibration setting back to low. The well-dressed lawyer occasionally glanced up at me, darting his eyes back and forth between my tight bosom and my bare knees under the table. Hannah smiled when she recognized his attention as she toggled the remote control vibration settings in the palm of her hand.

While the pleasurable sensations began to spread over my pelvic region, I struggled to keep myself still in my seat watching Hannah's slit widening as she spread her legs further apart. When she suddenly turned on the clitoral vibration setting, I emitted a little squeak, and the young blonde girl looked up at me, pursing her lips to say "*Shhh!*"

"Sorry," I whispered, rubbing my hand over my exposed belly. "I've got a bit of an upset stomach."

She shook her head and returned to reading her book. But the direct stimulation on my clit had dramatically increased my pleasure and my knees began to part unconsciously. The handsome hunk looked up from his law books when he noticed the movement and peered under the table as I struggled to keep my knees from fluttering in excitement.

Hannah noticed the dynamic going on between the two of us, and when the hunk temporarily looked back down, she reached into the pocket of her dress and pulled out a long rubber dildo. As I watched her with glassy eyes, she slowly inserted the dong into her snatch and began to stroke it in and out of her hole. I shook my head at her to show my anger at her tormenting me, but she smiled back at me, sensuously licking her lips. She knew how much I liked to trib using a double-sided dildo, and as she rocked her hips slowly under the table, she took her hand off the shaft while the other end wobbled tantalizing in my direction.

I mouthed the words *Fuck You*, and she responded by saying *Yes Please*. As much as I tried to resist it, as she began to increase the speed of the clitoral massager, my legs continued to spread apart with a mind of their own. Before long, the handsome lawyer looked up at me again, this time his gaze squarely focused between my legs.

I knew he could probably see me just as well as I could see Hannah an equal distance away, and his eyes widened when he saw the strange blue device planted between my legs. Suddenly, he brought his hand under the table to adjust himself, and I noticed his pole tenting in his pants. As his lengthening hard-on snaked up the front of his hips, I dribbled down the side of my legs, admiring his impressive package. I grunted unconsciously watching his visceral reaction, and the pretty co-ed sitting next to me looked up again, shaking her head.

"Why don't you go to the *washroom* if you're not feeling well?" she said. "This is a library!"

"I'm sorry," I said, clutching my stomach. "I think it's something I ate. I'll be finished my research soon, then I'll leave."

The girl looked at my trembling tummy suspiciously, then returned to reading her book. When I peered over again at the hunky lawyer, I saw that he'd unzipped his pants, with his large dick poking straight up toward the underside of his table. Nobody else could have seen what he was doing from my vantage point, and he smiled at me as I spread my legs wider apart in sympathy. Part of me wanted to close my knees and hide the vibrator rumbling inside me, but when I saw him reach under the table and begin to stroke his cock, I couldn't help groaning as I imagined myself planted on top of him.

The girl looked up again, but seeing the strange look on my face as I peered at the hunk across the aisle, she traced my gaze over to him and gasped when she saw what he was doing under the table. After pausing for a moment, she looked back at me and smiled as she lowered her arm under the table and began to move her hand between her legs. I glanced over at Hannah and saw the big rubber dildo glistening from her juices while she watched the three-way action that was happening between our two tables.

As much as I tried to ignore the rising passion emanating from my twitching pussy, it was impossible to avoid the sight of the three beauties stimulating themselves while they watched me squirm and moan with the U-shaped vibrator stimulating every part of my dripping crotch. As the handsome hunk began jerking himself more forcefully under the table, my gaze shifted back to the pretty co-ed, whose cheeks were beginning to flush from the pleasure she was experiencing under the table. With the four of us nearing a mutual crescendo, I suddenly flashed back to my childhood, when my grandmother used to read bedtime stories to me.

Goodnight moon, I said to myself, trying to remember the words to my favorite story in an effort to shift my focus away from erotic scene unfolding before me. *Good night, cow jumping over the moon.*

When I refocused my gaze, I saw Hannah slumping in her chair with her legs spread wide apart, reaming herself with two hands tightly gripped around the shaft of the glistening dildo.

Good night kittens, good night mittens, I said to myself, trying to think of anything other than the sight of these three hotties rimming themselves in the middle of the public library. Whether each of them was fully aware of what the other was doing, from my perspective the sight of them pleasuring themselves together was impossible to resist.

I glanced at the pretty co-ed, and she looked me straight in the eye as a bright flush spread over her cheeks. When I turned back toward the hunky lawyer, he suddenly stopped moving his hand as he gripped his purple crown in his fist, spewing long ropes of cum all over the underside of the table.

Good night, bear. Good night, chairs, I murmured quickly under my breath.

When the girl saw the guy spurting cum out of his huge dick, she hunched over and gasped, jerking rhythmically in her seat. Seeing the other two coming so hard only a few feet away from me, Hannah groaned softly as she pulled the rubber dildo deep into her pussy, flapping her knees uncontrollably.

Good night, stars. Good night, air. Good night, noises everywhere, I said, feeling my juices streaming steadily down the insides of my legs.

5

———

"**N**o *fair!*" I protested when Hannah and I left the library. "You get to have all the fun while I suffer in silence!"

"I never said *I* couldn't come while you were doing these tests," Hannah smiled. "That's half the attraction. Nothing turns me on more than watching you twist and squirm while I stimulate you from a distance."

"*Give* me that fucking thing," I said, tearing the remote control device from her hand. "I don't want to wait another second to get off."

"Right *here*?" Hannah said, looking around the library entrance at the passing patrons.

"Why not? I've already had sex in two public places. What difference will it make if I do it *outside*?"

I peered around me and saw a small alcove near an emergency exit behind a stand of bushes.

"There's a relatively secluded spot over there. You can be my lookout."

"Fuck that," Hannah said, grabbing my hand, pulling me behind the hedge. "I want a piece of this too."

We ducked into the doorway, pressing our bodies together and I flicked on the remote control switch. Hannah reached down and pulled the vibrator out of my pussy, then reinserted each end into our separate holes.

"There's more than *one* way to use this flexible toy," she smiled.

"Except *this* time," I said, "I'll be in charge of controlling the level of stimulation."

I tapped the two buttons on the controller then adjusted the flywheels to their maximum setting. Hannah lifted the front of our skirts and pressed her mound against mine, kissing me passionately. Even though I only had half of the U-shaped vibrator throbbing against me, the action of Hannah's mound grinding up against my own provided more than enough clitoral stimulation. As we thrust our tongues into each other's mouths, I reached under Hannah's dress and grabbed her buttocks, pulling her hard against me.

"I'm going to cum all over your little twat," I said, feeling my orgasm rising within me like a powerful volcano.

"Let it go, girl," Hannah said.

I lifted my knee and wrapped my leg around her ass, pointing my vulva against her mound.

"Uhnn," I groaned. "Here it comes. *Fuckkkk!*"

As my pussy clamped down over the fat end of the vibrator, I squirted my pent-up juices out the sides of my slit all over Hannah's abdomen as we shook in each other's arms from the combined stimulation of the curved wand.

"*Fuck me,*" Hannah said as we collapsed against the side of the door with our juices streaming down the insides of our legs. "I never even thought about using this as a double-sided dildo."

"How do *you* like not being in control for a change?" I said, raising my eyebrows in protest. "Now you know what I've been going through these last two episodes."

"I have a whole new respect for what you've been able to accomplish," she nodded. "Especially with those two hotties jerking off right next to you."

"You have no idea," I said. "That hunk sitting next to you was hung like a horse. You should have seen him when he finally dumped his load. I thought he'd never stop coming underneath the desk."

"I guess the clean-up crew will have more than a few wads of gum to scrape of the bottom of the table next time," Hannah chuckled. "But I was more focused on the cute girl sitting beside you. She certainly changed her tune when she finally figured out what was going on."

"When I saw the sex flush roll over her cheeks, it took every ounce of my willpower not to come along with her."

"How *did* you manage to keep it together?" Hannah asked. "I thought you were really going to lose control this time."

"I just transported myself somewhere else and tried to think of something as far removed from my predicament as possible."

"Well, whatever it was, it seemed to work. Though I dare say the three of *us* more than made up for your lack of enthusiasm. I haven't come that hard in ages."

"So what now?" I said. "Now that I've managed to get the hotel and airfare paid for, what do I have to do to cover the meals for our trip to Bora Bora?"

Hannah pulled the vibrator out of our pussies and leaned against the opposite wall of the alcove as she looked at me with a sly smile.

"We have to step it *up* another notch, right? Both of these times you were fully clothed and had a few props to distract attention from what was going on down there. This next time, you're going to be completely *naked*."

I shook my head and peered at her with a quizzical look.

"Are you taking me to a nude beach or something?"

"Even better," she smirked. "You're going to be a nude model for a college art class."

"What the–" I gasped, feeling my pussy twitch one last time, sending another stream of juices running down my leg.

For the next week or so, all I could think about was what it would be like to stand in front of a group of strangers while they sketched me in the nude. As much as I tried to get more details from

Hannah, she refused to give me any more information until we arrived at the studio. I wasn't exactly sure how she was going to pull off stimulating me from a distance with a vibrator sticking out of my pussy. But every time I thought about it, I stood in front of my full-length dressing mirror imagining everyone watching me while I jilled myself to orgasm.

On the scheduled appointment day, Hannah drove me to the local college, where we met with the art professor to go over the ground rules for the session. The prof was younger and prettier than I imagined, and I sat in rapt attention while she explained how it all worked.

"Hi, I'm Danielle," she said, introducing herself to the two of us.

"Jade," I said, extending my hand.

"Hannah," my partner-in-crime said.

"Which one of you will be posing today?"

I held up my hand meekly.

"I'm just here for moral support," Hannah smiled.

"The protocol is pretty straight-forward," Danielle said. "We'll keep you covered up until everyone is ready to begin. Then I'll ask you to hold a pose for about thirty minutes while the students draw you in the nude. I'll be circulating around the room during this time, offering feedback and critique on their compositions. The most important thing is for you to try to remain as still as possible for the duration of the assignment."

While she was talking to the two of us, I stole occasional glances at her figure. She was wearing a tight-fitting mid-length skirt and a white cotton blouse partially unbuttoned at the neck. Her breasts were full and round, and my gaze kept falling to her sexy cleavage and her toned legs crossed at the knee. By the time she finished her briefing, I could feel the heat emanating from my throbbing pussy.

"Did you have any questions?" she asked.

"How many people are we expecting to show up?" I asked nervously.

"We have twenty students in my class, and I expect most of them to show up for this assignment. This is one of the more popular electives."

"I can see why," Hannah said, eyeing my curvy figure under my robe.

"And I can't cover up any part of my body?" I said.

"That's the whole point of figure drawing," Danielle said. "To sketch the subject in his or her full glory."

"Don't people sometimes get–um–*excited* with so many eyes on their naked body?" I said, wondering especially how a male model would manage to keep himself composed in this situation.

"I tell both the models and the artists that it's perfectly normal and natural. That's part of the challenge–to capture their feelings and emotions in a still composition."

"May I participate in the session also?" Hannah asked. "I mean as an *artist*. I've always wanted to sketch Jade in the nude."

"Of course," Danielle said. "I only ask that you try not to distract the model with any overt comments or expressions."

"I wouldn't *dream* of it," Hannah smiled.

"Okay," the professor said. "Why don't you take a few minutes to freshen up and prepare yourself while the students get set up?"

Hannah and I walked out into the hallway where we found a private washroom, locking the door behind us.

"Okay," I said, crossing my arms impatiently. "How exactly are you going to pull this off with everyone staring at my naked pussy?"

"Never fear, my pretty," Hannah cooed, taking a small dumbbell-shaped object out of her purse. "These are a special type of Ben-wa balls. They vibrate in different ways, depending on how I adjust the controller. Everything's going to be hiding *inside* you this time. No one will be any the wiser as to what's going on, unless you give them reason to suspect otherwise."

"Ben-wa balls," I nodded, reflecting back on the time I'd used them in the airplane lavatory with my Swedish stewardess friends. "Ingenious."

"You shouldn't have any trouble controlling yourself with *these* things, right?" Hannah said, raising a playful eyebrow. "Only one *part* of you is going to be stimulated this time."

"Well, as you've explained to me many times, the main body of my clitoris is actually located on the *inside* of my vagina, not the outside. And I've already had some experience with these things. So *no*, it's not going to be any easier to control myself."

"Well this should be all the more interesting then," Hannah smiled, reaching under my robe and inserting the chrome balls into my slit.

When we returned to the studio, the classroom had already filled up with students, and the instructor motioned for everyone to take their seats. There was an even mix of men and women, and they were all young and cute. As Danielle introduced me to the class, I scanned around the room, feeling my pussy throb as I made eye contact with each student.

In the front row, a pretty brunette with a cute ponytail smiled at me as I glanced at her tawny thighs exposed in cut-off jeans under her tilted drafting table. Directly behind her, a cute redhead with little freckles sprinkled over her nose peered up at me, gazing at my excited nipples poking two darts in the soft fabric of my robe. As I traced a line further toward the back of the room, I saw an African-American man looking like a young Denzel Washington nodding at me as he admired my curvy figure.

Fuck me, I thought. *They're not going to make this any easier for me.*

As I imagined fucking each one of them in turn, the professor interrupted my thoughts with final instructions to the group.

"Because of the personal nature of this session, I'll ask everyone to place their phones in their pockets or purses to protect the privacy of our subject. You all know the protocol for drawing the model, which I've already explained to Jade, so if you'd like to take out your drawing materials now, we can begin. Jade, if you feel comfortable, you may disrobe now and sit comfortably on the stool."

The professor motioned to an adjacent chair, and I pulled off my robe and sat awkwardly on the bench with my feet propped up on the lower bar and my knees clamped tightly together.

"You may wish to turn your body a few degrees to your left," Danielle instructed, "so our students can depict a partial side profile. Try to relax your legs by placing one foot on the floor and the other on the lower foot rest. As far as your hands, most models find it most comfortable to rest them in their lap. Since we'll need you to remain as still as possible for the duration of the session, you may find it useful to find a focal point somewhere in the room where you can fix your gaze. Are we ready to begin?"

I nodded my head and scanned the back wall, seeing a message board above the African-American student's head. A sign listed the ten meeting norms to optimize productivity, and I began to read them quietly to myself to distract attention from the twenty sets of eyes starting at my naked body.

Show up on time and come prepared, the first rule said.

Check, I said to myself. *Although I'm not sure coming to class with two steel balls embedded in my pussy qualifies exactly as 'prepared'.*

Suddenly, I felt the balls begin to tremble inside me, and I shifted uncomfortably on my chair.

Stay mentally and physically present, the second rule said.

I'm physically present alright, but my *mind* is definitely elsewhere.

I drew my focus back about ten feet, noticing the cute brunette in the front row swinging her legs as she slowly etched her pencil over her drawing pad. In my periphery, I could see the white fringes on the bottom of her shorts flapping over her inner thighs, and I wondered if she was doing it to help focus on her drawing, or if it was because she was getting aroused by my naked body.

I could feel my nipples hardening as I watched her hands moving over the canvas, wondering what it would feel like to have her touch my *real* body. Hannah must have noticed my distraction, because I could feel the movement of the Ben-wa balls steadily increasing inside my pussy. Suddenly, I was mindful of how wet the chrome seat under my ass had become, feeling the tip of my clit dip into the little puddle I'd created in the concave surface of the stool. As she dialed up the vibration of the two balls shaking inside me, the radiating forces on the underside of my vulva made little ripples in the fluid, splashing gently back and forth over my tingling bulb.

Great, I grimaced. *Just what I need right now. Yet another form of uncontrolled stimulation to my most sensitive body part.*

I was tempted to lower my pinky under my resting palms to stimulate my aching clit, then I remembered the purpose of this exercise was to *contain* my pleasure not encourage it.

Contribute to the meeting goals, the third rule on the sign said.

Check, I said, clenching my buttock cheeks to fight off the rising passion.

I adjusted my focus to the pretty redhead in the same line of sight and noticed her cheeks flushing over her pale skin. For a moment, I imagined what it would be like to suck on her pretty pussy while I watched a deeper flush roll over her naked chest.

Get it together Jade, I said to myself, glancing up at the clock on the wall. *You only need to get through another fifteen minutes, then you can fantasize all you want about fucking these cuties.*

My eyes drifted back to the sign above Denzel Washington's head, reading the fourth rule.

Let everyone participate, it instructed.

I peered down a few inches, noticing his arm muscles flexing as he brushed his fingers over his canvas.

I bet he knows how to please a woman with those soft hands of his, I fantasized.

Suddenly I felt the two chrome balls begin to flex back and forth, caressing the walls of my dripping pussy. While they pounded inside me, I imagined his cock sliding in and out of my hole as I gripped his powerful arms.

Fuck, Hannah, I cursed under my breath. It was almost like she was reading my mind, adjusting the action of the Ben-wa balls to mimic the fantasies that were racing through my mind.

With the pleasurable sensations steadily building inside my womb, I could feel my breathing increasing as my breasts began to rise and fall on my chest. Surely everyone must have noticed my internal distraction, and I half expected the teacher to admonish me to remain still. But she was too busy circulating among the group to pay any attention to me. When she angled back toward the front of the room, she bent over to observe the brunette's work, and I gawked at her fleshy breasts, barely supported by the flimsy fabric of her blouse.

God damn, I murmured. *I'd love to bury my face in those tits. Or better yet, rub my cunt against her melons while she watched me squirt all over her body.*

As my body continued to heave unconsciously on my stool, my clit dipped in and out of the increasingly large puddle I was forming on the seat, and I clenched my jaw trying to stifle my rising passion.

I glanced back up at the wall clock and noticed I only had five minutes left to finish my test. Recognizing my increasing distress, Hannah flicked her thumbs over the remote control and suddenly I felt the Ben-was balls begin to *rotate* on their axis.

Oh my God, I panted under my breath. *What else can these evil things do?*

By now, I was being silently fucked by the three-way action of the miniature dumbbells. In addition to flexing back and forth, they were twirling inside me like a slingshot, while rotating rapidly. The combined stimulation on the walls of my pussy was almost unbearable.

I could see my thigh muscles clenching as I stiffened my body trying to fight back the rising wall of pleasure, but just as I was about to pop off, the teacher stood up and told everyone to put their pencils down. Suddenly, the whirring balls stopped moving inside me and I relaxed my buttock muscles, feeling my burning lips dip back down into the warm puddle beneath me.

"Okay everyone," Danielle announced. "Time's up. Please stop sketching and bring your completed compositions to the front of the room before you leave. Jade, you may put on your robe now. Thank you for your time and participation in today's art class. We have a small parting gift for you before you leave. Next week, we have a *sculpture* class scheduled. If you'd like to come back and join us again, we'd love to have you."

I pulled the robe back over my shoulders, then Danielle handed me a long cardboard tube and thanked me again for my participation.

"If you'd like to model for us again, please let me know," she said, clasping my shaking hand. "You seem to have inspired a whole new level of dedication in my students' craft."

Later that day when I got home and opened the tube, I pulled out a long piece of parchment paper. Sketched on the front was a picture of me with my head thrown back in the throes of passion with my hands positioned in front of my snatch between my outspread legs. But instead of the stool I was sitting on in class, I was sitting on a giant, stylized chrome dildo, deeply embedded in my pussy. The signature on the bottom of the sketch simply read *Han.*

I smiled, admiring the surreal illustration.

"I didn't know you could draw, you little devil," I said.

Then I pulled my favorite rabbit vibrator out of my nightstand and rammed it inside me, beginning to dream of what fantasy Hannah had in store for me next.

6

———

"I can't *imagine* what you have planned for this final test," I said to Hannah when she came to pick me up a few days later. "What could be more difficult than having to stand motionless for thirty minutes while you stimulate me completely naked in front of twenty sexy college students?"

"That was pretty hot," Hannah nodded. "You definitely earned your choice of five-star restaurants on our little getaway to Bora Bora."

"What's my motivation for this last challenge?" I said. "Everything's already pretty much paid for. What's stopping me from just enjoying myself and letting it all go?"

"How does a snorkeling expedition to swim with the sharks and rays in the crystalline waters of an off-shore reef sound?"

"Not as dangerous as what I suspect you've got cooked up for me today."

"What about a catamaran cruise to our own private island for a candlelight dinner under the stars?"

"That's definitely on my bucket list..."

"Or a full-day spa treatment with hot stone massage, deep-clean facial, and sensuous body scrub?"

"Okay, *fine*, you little bugger," I chuckled. "You've twisted my arm. So, what have you got in store for me today?"

Hannah paused as her mouth curled up on one side.

"Watching you try to recite the prayers while I stimulated you at the church got me thinking. That was almost too *easy* with everyone looking the other way. At this *next* venue, everyone's going to be hanging on your every word..."

"What–am I going to be giving some kind a speech or something?"

"Almost," she smiled. "You're going to be reading a book for some of my book club friends."

"What's the book?"

"Delta of Venus, by Anais Nin."

"I've heard of that," I nodded. "Isn't that the one with all the steamy vignettes describing the author's sexual escapades?"

"Yes."

"So let me get this straight," I said. "You want me to read a story describing graphic sex without getting aroused while you stimulate me from a distance with a secret vibrator?"

"Exactly."

I shook my head, hardly believing the lengths Hannah had gone to to dream up these outrageous scenarios.

"Who will be my audience?"

"It's an LGBT book club, so it'll be a group of about twenty young women–"

"You've *got* to be kidding me," I said. "You expect me to remain composed while I'm reading a sex scene surrounded by a bunch of hot lesbians?"

"If you want the spa and the cruise and the snorkeling expedition..." she smirked.

"You are *truly* an evil witch, you know that, right?"

"That's why you love me so much," Hannah said, rubbing up against me playfully.

"And where exactly is this latest excursion going to take place?" I said, wondering what else she was planning to raise the stakes.

"At the local bookstore. They have a little coffee shop in the back which they allow our group to use from time to time."

"Great," I said, pushing her away in disgust. "So you're going to be diddling me as an untold number of strangers walk in and out of the coffee shop?"

"Mmm-hmm," Hannah nodded.

"Will you be using Ben-wa balls again, since I'll be exposed to the public?"

"Oh *no*," Hannah said, shaking her head teasingly. "We'll have to make this a little more interesting if you want to pass the ultimate test."

"You've already subjected me to the dual action of the *We-Vibe* vibrator. What could possibly be more stimulating than that?"

Hannah reached into her purse and pulled out a familiar finger-shaped toy.

"Not the *Osé* vibrator!" I squealed. "You're making this almost impossible! How do you expect me to control myself with a realistic finger and tongue caressing my private parts while I'm getting turned on reading a sexy story to a bunch of sexy women?"

"*You're* the one who bragged about how easily you can turn it on and off," Hannah shrugged. "If you pass this final test, I'll give you whatever you want."

"If I pass this test," I said, crossing my arms indignantly, "I'll expect Scarlett Johansson as my personal masseuse and Thomas Keller as our chef!"

"I'll see what I can arrange..."

When we got to the bookstore, Hannah set me up on a comfortable settee with a small reading table. On its surface rested a hardcover book with an image of a half-naked woman kneeling on an upholstered chair with her legs splayed in a sexy pose.

At least I'll be reasonably covered up this time, I thought, beginning to get aroused looking at the provocative picture.

Hannah had allowed me to wear a loose-fitting summer dress that concealed most of my body, but she'd insisted I go au naturel underneath to permit maximum freedom of movement for both me and the vibrator. As the book club members began to wander into the bookstore, she introduced me to each one in turn, and I was struck by how young and pretty they all were. It was far cry from the collection of frumpy nerds I'd half-expected. When everybody had assembled in the lounge, she stood up to address the group while I tried to compose myself by straightening out my dress over my shaking knees.

"Welcome to the monthly meeting of the Literary Coven book group," Hannah said. "Today I've invited a special guest to read a passage from one of my favorite erotic books, Delta of Venus, by Anais Nin. She's kindly, um, *volunteered* to read a chapter I think you'll find quite stimulating and moving. So without any further ado, I give you my friend, Jade."

The women clapped softly while they examined my naked shoulders and legs as I smiled back at them politely. I shifted my weight to the edge of the settee and picked up the book, turning to the bookmarked chapter, titled *Elena*.

The three women met, I read softly, *driven inside the same cafe on a day of heavy rain...*

I had no idea when Hannah would begin her private stimulation of me and the anticipation made the reading all the more tension-filled.

Leila, perfumed and dashing, carrying her head high, a silver fox stole undulating around her shoulders over her trim black suit...

What beautiful prose, I thought to myself, already beginning to lose myself in the story.

Elena, in a wine-colored velvet, and Bijou, in her streetwalker's costume, which she could never abandon, the tight-fitting black dress and high-heeled shoes.

Interesting premise, I said to myself. I was already hooked, beginning to understand the attraction of sharing a well-written book with a collection of like-minded women. I glanced over at Hannah, who was peering at me with a devilish look in her eyes.

Suddenly, I felt the long finger of the Osé vibrator beginning to flex inside my pussy, and I squirmed on my seat trying to distract myself from the humanlike sensation.

Leila smiled at Bijou, I said, pausing to collect my breath, *then recognized Elena. Shivering, the three of them sat down before aperitifs.*

As I continued reading the story, Hannah slowly ramped up the vibration of the undulating finger caressing the walls of my pussy while I struggled to maintain my composure.

What Elena had not expected, I shuddered, *was to be completely intoxicated with Bijou's voluptuous charm. On her right sat Leila, incisive, brilliant, and on her left, Bijou, like a bed of sensuality Elena wanted to fall into.*

While I read the exquisitely written book, I found myself getting increasingly pulled into the story, imagining myself in the role of Elena, surrounded by the two fascinating women. When the story took a sexy turn, I found my body reacting as if I were right there with them.

The first one to move was Leila, I read, looking up to see a pretty blonde staring squarely into my eyes. *Who slid her jeweled hand under Bijou's skirt and gasped slightly with surprise at the unexpected touch of flesh where she had expected to find silky underwear.*

I paused for a moment to take a drink of water. The group nodded at me softly, recognizing my silent torment.

Leila had a moment of jealousy, I read, gulping down the last bit of water in my mouth. *Each caress she gave to Bijou, Bijou transmitted to Elena—the very same caress.*

I jerked suddenly in my seat and closed my eyes, feeling the pleasurable sensations from the undulating wand beginning to wash over me.

"Sorry," I said, looking up. "I guess I'm getting more attached to this story than I expected."

"Don't worry," one of the girls whispered. "We're enjoying your rendition. We've never had someone read a book so...*passionately*."

I peered over at Hannah, who was looking at me with a wicked grin. I cleared my throat, feeling the lips of my vulva moistening with a light dew.

After Leila kissed Bijou's luxuriant mouth, I read, turning the page, *Bijou took Elena's lips between her own. When Leila's hand slipped further under Bijou's dress*–huh! I gasped, feeling a wave of pleasure roll over me–*Bijou slid her hand under Elena's. Elena, seeing Bijou offered, dared to touch her voluptuous body, following every contour of her rich curves...*

As I continued reading the erotic story, my hips began to move unconsciously on the dimpled settee, mimicking the action of the characters in the story. I could feel the moisture beginning to pour out of me as the pendulous finger probed deep inside my hole. Coffee shop patrons paused briefly to peer over at me, pinching their eyebrows trying to imagine why I was so immersed in the story.

A bed of down, soft, firm flesh without bones, I read haltingly, *smelling of sandalwood and musk. Her own nipples hardened as she touched Bijou's breasts.*

Suddenly I became aware of how the *rest* of my body was responding as I read the sexy tale. With my bare nipples rubbing against the soft cotton fabric of my dress, every hair on my body was standing on end, as goose bumps covered every square inch of my skin.

When her hand passed around Bijou's buttocks–huh, huh, huh, I spasmed quietly on the sofa–*it met Leila's hand.*

At this point I still only had the internal part of the vibrator moving against me, and I shuddered to think how I would keep it together if and when Hannah turned on the other half of the device. As the action in the story continued to ramp up, so did the pleasure continuing to build unabated in my twitching pussy.

Leila began to undress, I panted, *exposing a soft little black satin corse-let, which held her stockings with tiny black garters. Her thighs...slender and white, gleamed...her sex lay in shadow.*

Fuck me, I thought, picturing the scene like I was right there. *This is an incredibly erotic story. To hell with reading this in public–as soon as I get home, I'm going to rip off my clothes and enjoy this properly in the privacy of my own bedroom.*

Hannah suddenly peered up at me, reading my thoughts, and I felt the snake-like appendage hidden in the *other* end of the vibrator begin to press up against my burning clit.

Oh God, I panted under my breath, trying to steel myself against the rising passion beginning to consume my body.

Leila pressed Bijou onto her side, I hissed, *with one leg thrown over Leila's shoulder. And she was kissing Bijou between her–uhn–legs.*

While I read the increasingly bawdy scene, my face contorted in a series of pained expressions as I tried to ignore the animatronic appendages caressing both sides of my pussy.

Now and then...Bijou jerked backwards...away from the stinging kisses and bites, the tongue that was as hard as a man's sex.

Hannah must have chosen this passage explicitly, knowing how much it would torture me to read a passage mirroring the action of the device whirring and shaking against my vulva. As I continued reading the story, she modulated the type and intensity of the device's movement to match precisely how the characters were interacting.

With her hands, Elena had been enjoying the shape of Bijou's body, and now she inserted her finger into the tight little aperture...

I groaned out loud, feeling the disembodied finger beginning to caress the front of my G-spot.

There she could feel, I moaned, *every contraction caused by Leila's kisses–uhn–as if she were touching the wall against which Leila moved her tongue.*

As the fleshy tongue of the Osé vibrator rolled over my tingling clit, I felt myself beginning to lose control. The wall of pleasure rising within me was like a riptide, pushing back against my feeble attempt to resist the flow.

When she was about to come and could no longer defend herself against her pleasure–uh, uh, I heaved–Leila stopped kissing her, leaving Bijou halfway on the peak of an excruciating sensation, half-crazed.

Recognizing that I was on the verge of coming, Hannah simultaneously stopped the vibrator, and I looked up at her with a start.

Please, I mouthed to her, asking her to release me from my torment. She held up her finger up and twirled it in circles, instructing me to finish the chapter. I closed my eyes, taking a deep breath, and resumed reading.

Uncontrollable now, I gasped, *like some magnificent maniac, Bijou threw herself over Elena's body, parted her legs, placed herself between them, glued her sex to Elena's and moved, moved with desperation.*

Yes, I whispered softly, desperate to consummate my own pleasure along with my new imaginary friends.

Elena was now in the frenzy before climax, I cackled, feeling both parts of the vibrator starting up inside me again. *She felt a hand under her, a hand she could rub against. She wanted to throw herself on it until it made her come, but she also wanted to prolong her pleasure.*

Hannah turned down the motion of the finger thrusting inside me again, and I cursed her under my breath.

So she ceased moving, but the hand pursued her, I grunted. *She stood up, and the hand again traveled towards her sex...*

Possessed of another spirit, I slowly rose out of my chair, cradling the book in two hands as streams of lubrication trickled down the inside of my thighs below the hem of my dress.

Then she felt Bijou standing against her back, panting. She felt the pointed breasts, the brushing of Bijou's sexual hair against her buttocks.

As I read the captivating text, my *own* body began to sway and undulate against my literary lover.

Bijou rubbed against her, knowing the friction would force Elena to turn so as to feel this on her breasts, sex, and belly. Elena's body was so burning hot that she feared one more touch would set off the explosion. Leila sensed this, and the two of them together attacked Bijou, intent on drawing from her the ultimate sensation.

Fuck yes, I panted out loud.

She was begging now to be satisfied, spread her legs, sought to satisfy herself by friction against the others' bodies. With tongues and fingers, they pried into her, back and front, sometimes stopping to touch each other's tongue–Elena and Leila, mouth to mouth, tongues curled together, over Bijou's spread legs.

"*Oh God*", I squealed, feeling my climax beginning to overtake me. *Fuck the massage and the snorkeling expedition*, I said to myself. *I need to be taken right now.*

As I read the final passage of the chapter, my hips began to shake while I struggled to hold the book in my hands.

Bijou's orgasm came like an exquisite torment, I read. *At each spasm, she moved as if she were being stabbed.*

Suddenly, the walls of my pussy clamped down hard and I gushed like a waterfall onto the hard wooden floor beneath me. Every one of the book club members gasped, realizing what was happening to me, then silence filled the room as I stood trembling in the throes of the most powerful orgasm I could remember.

When I finally put the book down, I looked up at them meekly. They stared at me for a long moment, still in shock at what they'd just witnessed, then they all stood up, clapping loudly in unison. As I smiled back at them, feeling the cool sticky moisture between my legs, I glanced over at Hannah and she nodded toward me, joining the others in applause.

I shook my head in amazement, realizing I'd earned every piece of her promised prize.

R eady for more erotic chills and thrills? Preorder the next volume in the Erotica Themed Bundles series, *Ladyboys 2 (coming soon)*.

What could be more fun than having it both ways?

ALSO BY VICTORIA RUSH

Adult Fairytales:

The Enchanted Forest: An Erotic Fairytale

The Land of Giants: An Erotic Fairytale

The Dragon's Lair: An Erotic Fairytale

Witch's Brew: An Erotic Fairytale

The Mage's Spell: An Erotic Fairytale

The Mermaid Lagoon: An Erotic Fairytale

The Coven: An Erotic Fairytale

Rapunzel: An Erotic Fairytale

The Seven Dwarfs: An Erotic Fairytale

The Land of Mutants: An Erotic Fairytale

The Erotic Temple: A Sexy Fairytale (Coming Soon)

Erotica Themed Bundles:

Voyeur: Lesbian Erotica Bundle

Public Affairs: A Lesbian Anthology

Futa Fantasies: The Ladyboy Collection

Threesomes: The Lesbian Collection

Threesomes - Volume 2: The Lesbian Collection

First Time: A Lesbian Anthology

Hedonism: An Erotic Anthology

Switch Hitters: Bisexual Erotica

Taboo Erotica: The Lesbian Series

BDSM: The Lesbian Collection

Party Games: The Erotic Collection

Party Games 2: The Erotic Collection

All Girl 1: Lesbian Erotica Bundle

All Girl 2: Lesbian Erotica Bundle

All Girl 3: Lesbian Erotica Bundle

All Girl 4: Lesbian Erotica Bundle

Erotic Fairytale Bundles:

Clover's Fantasy Adventures: Books 1 - 5

Clover's Fantasy Adventures: Books 6 - 10

Erotic Fantasy:

Pirate's Bounty: A Time Travel Adventure

Wild West: A Time Travel Adventure

Private Riley: A Time Travel Adventure

Cleopatra's Secret: A Time Travel Adventure

Bounty Hunter 2125: A Time Travel Adventure

Ninja Assassin: A Time Travel Adventure

The 300: A Time Travel Adventure

Arabian Nights: An Erotic Fairytale (coming soon...)

Steamy Time Travel Bundles:

Riley's Time Travel Adventures: Books 1 - 5

Lesbian Erotica:

The Dinner Party: Lesbian Voyeur Erotica

The Darkroom: Bisexual Voyeur Erotica

Naked Yoga: Lesbian Transgender Erotica

Nude Cruise: Bisexual Voyeur Erotica

Rush Hour: Taboo Public Sex

The Girl Next Door: First Time Lesbian Erotic Romance

Girls' Camp: Lesbian Group Sex

Wet Dream: Ladyboy Fantasy Erotica

The Convent: Taboo Sex with a Nun

Sex Robot: A Dream Sex Machine

The Personal Trainer: Getting Pumped at the Gym

The Dominatrix: BDSM Lesbian Domination

Webcam Chat: Lesbian Online Sex

Paint Me: A Kinky Bodypainting Workshop

The Toy Party: Girls Sharing Sex Toys

The Costume Party: Strapping One On

Swedish Sauna: Lesbian Group Sex

The Therapist: Taboo Lesbian Erotica

Elevator Shaft: Bisexual Threesomes Erotica

Ladyboy: Lesbian Transgender Erotica

Peep Show: Lesbian Voyeur Erotica

The Dare: Public Sex Erotica

Maid Service: Lesbian Threesomes Erotica

The Hitchhiker: First Time Lesbian Erotica

The Housesitter: Spycam Lesbian Erotica

The Spa: Lesbian Group Orgy

Parlor Games: Blindfold Sex Party

The Exchange Student: First Time Lesbian Erotica

The Hostel: Bisexual Group Erotica

The Harem: Lesbian Erotic Romance

The Orient Express: Lesbian Voyeur Erotica

The First Lady: A Forbidden Lesbian Erotic Romance

The Slave: Lesbian BDSM Erotica

The Masseuse: Lesbian Sensuous Erotica

Too Close for Comfort: Lesbian Forbidden Erotica

Naked Twister: A Wild Party Game

Lexi: The Sex App (Lesbian Fantasy Erotica)

Call Girl: Lesbian Bisexual Threesomes Erotica

Circle Jill: Lesbian Masturbation Workshop

The Viewing Room: Masturbation Voyeur Erotica

Spin the Bottle: A Kinky Party Game

The Hair Salon: Lesbian Voyeur Erotica

Tribadism 1: Girls Only Sex Workshop

Tribadism 2: The Art of Scissoring

Tribadism 3: Threeway Hookups

The Kiss: A Game of Oral Sex

Pledge Week: Sorority Sisters

Carny Games 1: A Wild Sex Party

Carny Games 2: A Kinky Sex Party

Carny Games 3: An Erotic Sex Party

Dreamscape: An Artificial Reality Game

Glory Hole: Guess Who's On the Other Side

Joy Ride: A Late Night Erotic Bus Trip

The Blind Girl: An Erotic Romance(Coming Soon)

Lesbian Erotica Bundles:

Jade's Erotic Adventures: Books 1 - 5

Jade's Erotic Adventures: Books 6 - 10

Jade's Erotic Adventures: Books 11 - 15

Jade's Erotic Adventures: Books 16 - 20

Jade's Erotic Adventures: Books 21 - 25

Jade's Erotic Adventures: Books 26 - 30

Jade's Erotic Adventures: Books 31 - 35

Jade's Erotic Adventures: Books 36 - 40

Jade's Erotic Adventures: Books 41 - 45

Jade's Erotic Adventures: Books 46 - 50

Fifty Shades of Jade: Superbundle

Standalone Stories:

The Polynesian Girl: A Lesbian EroticRomance

FOLLOW VICTORIA RUSH:

Want to keep informed of my latest erotic book releases? Sign up for my newsletter and receive a FREE bonus book:

Spying on the neighbors just got a lot more interesting...

www.ingramcontent.com/pod-product-compliance
Lightning Source LLC
Chambersburg PA
CBHW032032310726
48972CB00002B/636